Nineteen Seventy

THE SEVEN BOOK ONE

SARAH M. CRADIT

Cover Design by Storyville Designs
Editing by Lawrence Editing

ISBN: 978-1-958744-24-6

Publisher Contact:
sarah@sarahmcradit.com
www.sarahmcradit.com

Foreword

Welcome to the Seventies. A time many would call the most formative and pivotal of the last hundred years, where the world was on the verge of everything. If you're my father, you'd say these first few years of the decade were the best time for music—ever. If you're a reader of my House of Crimson & Clover series, then you'll know that the '70s is when the mothers and fathers of the Crimson & Clover generation came of age themselves. Where they made the decisions that would shape a future full of love and pain in equal measure.

You don't need to have read The House of Crimson & Clover to read The Seven Series. This series stands on its own merits, a snapshot in fascinating time. In fact, I might even say that I'm envious of those readers who get to experience Colleen, Charles, and the others for the first time as the individuals they were before they were leading their own families. If you have read HoCC, you'll see how the characters you love in the present became who they are.

In full disclosure, I was not alive in the '70s. Although I was raised on the remnants of the era, including a steady diet of Crosby, Stills, & Nash, I did not live through this fascinating period in our history. To stay as true as possible to the era, I consulted many people who did—including my own father, George Klepach, who was truly a man of his time. Another valuable resource for me was photographer and author Deborah Burst, who not only came of age in this era, but in New Orleans, where this series comes to life. Also, to the many others I consulted in my crowd-sourcing who helped me to get the slang, clothing, food, and other things dialed in—I sincerely thank you. The internet was sometimes a great help, and other times not helpful at all, when it came to searching for what stores were on what streets, in what neighborhoods, in certain years. If there wasn't a Schwegmann's on Tchoupitoulas in 1970, for example, well, that's entirely my bad. I researched everything, but not everything had information available, so I made some educated guesses within context. As such, I want to be clear that any errors are entirely my own.

Since the day I penned the histories of this fascinating family, I've wanted to write this series. The origins of the seven Deschanel children, each distinctive in their own ways, has long been a part of the series canon, and now I'm sharing it with you. I adore origin stories, and hope you'll love this one as I do. Then again, I'm the reader who wishes J.K. Rowling would write that series about The Marauders already...

With all that said, enjoy the ride.

Also by Sarah M. Cradit

KINGDOM OF THE WHITE SEA

Kingdom of the White Sea Trilogy

The Kingless Crown

The Broken Realm

The Hidden Kingdom

The Book of All Things

Blackwood Cycle

The Raven and the Rush

The Poison and the Paladin

Southerlands Cycle

The Sylvan and the Sand

The Flame and the Forsaken

Guardians Cycle

The Altruist and the Assassin

The Belle and the Blackbird

Darkwood Cycle

The Melody and the Master

The Hand and the Heart

Sceptre Cycle

The Claw and the Crowned

The Duke and the Disciple

THE SAGA OF CRIMSON & CLOVER

The House of Crimson and Clover Series

The Storm and the Darkness

Shattered

The Illusions of Eventide

Bound

Midnight Dynasty

Asunder

Empire of Shadows

Myths of Midwinter

The Hinterland Veil

The Secrets Amongst the Cypress

Within the Garden of Twilight

House of Dusk, House of Dawn

Midnight Dynasty Series

A Tempest of Discovery

A Storm of Revelations

A Torrent of Deceit

The Seven Series

Nineteen Seventy

Nineteen Seventy-Two

Nineteen Seventy-Three

Nineteen Seventy-Four

Nineteen Seventy-Five

Nineteen Seventy-Six

Nineteen Eighty

Vampires of the Merovingi Series

The Island

and more

The Dusk Trilogy

St. Charles at Dusk: The Story of Oz and Adrienne

Flourish: The Story of Anne Fontaine

Banshee: The Story of Giselle Deschanel

Crimson & Clover Stories

Available as a single collection, The Shorts

Surrender: The Story of Oz and Ana

Shame: The Story of Jonathan St. Andrews

Fire & Ice: The Story of Remy & Fleur

Dark Blessing: The Landry Triplets

Pandora's Box: The Story of Jasper & Pandora

The Menagerie: Oriana's Den of Iniquities

A Band of Heather: The Story of Colleen and Noah

The Ephemeral: The Story of Autumn & Gabriel

Bayou's Edge: The Landry Triplets

For more information, and exciting bonus material, visit www.sarahmcradit.com

The Seven in 1970

Children of
August Deschanel (deceased) &
Colleen "Irish Colleen" Brady

Charles August Deschanel, Aged 20
Augustus Charles Deschanel, Aged 19
Colleen Amelia Deschanel, Aged 18
Madeline Colleen Deschanel, Aged 17
Evangeline Julianne Deschanel, Aged 16
Maureen Amelia Deschanel, Aged 14
Elizabeth Jeanne Deschanel, Aged 11

For Madeline

SPRING 1970

NEW ORLEANS, LOUISIANA

Prologue: Irish Colleen and the Seven

Colleen Deschanel, known as Irish Colleen to her family and friends, peeked her head into the bedrooms of her seven children at Oak Haven, one by one, as she did every night of her life.

When she swung the door open into the room of her oldest, Charles, she was met with an empty room and unmade bed. Of course he was gone. He was always gone, even when he was here. At what point would the shock of his perpetual absence become less acute? Would it ever not feel like disappointment, like failure? She sighed with her whole body. Whatever indiscretions littered Charles' life on this night, they weren't happening under this roof. Sometimes she wondered if it was simply better *not* to know.

Next, she checked on Augustus, whose face, softly glowing under a dim lamp, was pressed into one of his many business textbooks. He flashed her a brief, sweet smile before returning to his work. Augustus, who was far more like his father than Charles, who should have been the heir, but tradition reigned over reason.

Her boys, her only boys, could not be more different. Her heart ached for them both, for those differences, for much more.

At Colleen's room, she was not surprised to see her eldest daughter turned in for the night, her bedtime set to perfect precision. She didn't have to wake her to ask if her homework was finished, because she wouldn't be sleeping with any tasks uncompleted. Colleen, her easy one. Too easy. Easy lightened the stress, but it did not always find a path to happiness.

Madeline was next. Irish Colleen paused before knocking. If August were still alive, he would understand her hesitation. He would feel her fears and read them without word, fully understanding how one day she expected to open the door and find Madeline gone, never to return. Her late husband could read a person like that, and sometimes Irish Colleen hated the intrusion, but mostly she grudgingly appreciated how it meant she rarely had to explain herself.

But Madeline was there, sitting cross-legged on her bed, flipping through a stack of records. Still dressed, her bell bottoms sagged over the edge of her comforter, long past her gaudy platform heels. *You'll break your neck one day.* Madeline acknowledged her with a quick, sharp look, but the wounds of their last fight still burned too hot, and she dropped her eyes again.

Evangeline's snores carried into the hallway, echoing off the ancient oak of the old Victorian. Evangeline always slept like a rock, and Irish Colleen suspected it was because her daughter's brain exhausted her. She was a genius, tested and all, and Irish Colleen was not, so she did not know how to handle her curious, high-wired child with the wild hair and thoughts. There was no one to ask. No one to help.

Irish Colleen's hand paused on her bedroom door, and then she went on, to Maureen, who, like Madeline, was also not speaking to her at present. That God had blessed her with five girls was undoubtedly penance for her sins, but she loved them all, even when they couldn't find it within themselves to love her back.

Maureen was mercifully asleep, but Irish Colleen still blew a kiss across the air. Their thing, when they weren't too angry with one another to have a thing.

As always, Irish Colleen stopped last at Elizabeth. Her youngest, Lizzy, fell into the role of the consummate baby of the family without much effort. Her need for solitude troubled Irish Colleen, but not near as much as the moments Elizabeth clung to her, helpless and afraid. Every night was a roll of the dice as to what awaited when she came to tuck her in.

All her children possessed peculiar gifts, but none as potent or as tormented as Elizabeth's.

Moonlight spilled through the dormer window and onto the floor before her youngest daughter's room. This nightly sight often put Irish Colleen's anxious heart at ease. As a devout Catholic, she knew there were signs everywhere, and this was God telling her he would pick up in protecting Elizabeth where Irish Colleen's limits stretched beyond their earthly capability. God punished, but he also provided. Protected.

Irish Colleen slipped inside the bedroom. Her heart seized at the sight of Elizabeth sitting bolt upright in her bed, drenched in her own sweat. Her hair and nightgown clung to her, hitching in weird places. Her hands twisted in her lap as she rocked.

Lord, she is too young to carry such burdens. She's only eleven. This is no childhood.

But Elizabeth's burden was not a gift from God, and Irish Colleen knew that, just as her other children's abilities were not. An eleven-year-old who could divine the future was no blessing, but it was surely a curse. If Irish Colleen spent too long considering this, she knew precisely who sent such gifts.

"Mama." The words fell from Elizabeth's lips with hardly a sound.

"Baby." Irish Colleen gathered her sweet girl in her arms. With one hand, she lifted the soaking nightgown off Elizabeth's body, and with the other, she felt around in the drawer beside the bed for a clean shift. Elizabeth sat in limp retreat as her mother changed her like an infant, despite that her body had begun to shift beyond the innocence of childhood.

There was nothing she could do to dry the hair quickly, so she pulled in behind Elizabeth and went to work on braiding her long, thick hair. "Why didn't you call me in?"

"I knew you'd come." Elizabeth sagged in front of her.

Of course you did. "Do you want to talk about what happened today? At school?"

Elizabeth tensed. "Charles is in trouble."

Irish Colleen held her sigh. Diversions were common with Elizabeth, a defense mechanism that proved perpetually troublesome for her both in school and at home. "When is Charles not in some kind of trouble?" she said. "Unless you're telling me he's in immediate danger? Right this moment?" She stopped her fingers. "Is that what you're saying?"

Elizabeth hung her head. "No, Mama."

"No, I didn't think so." Irish Colleen resumed her plaiting. "I can tell, Lizzy, the difference between when you really see something and when you want me to stop asking questions. Right now, you want me to stop asking questions. Don't you?"

Elizabeth's chest heaved with a heavy sob.

"But we both know I would never be angry with you for something you can't control. Your teachers, the kids at school, they don't understand. But I do, Lizzy." *August, damn you. You died and left me to cultivate who they are, and when you were alive you never wanted to talk about it. You passed these gifts to them, and you should be the one having these talks. Guiding them through the pains.*

"Mrs. Larsen told me..." Elizabeth swallowed down her emotion and pulled her shoulders back. Irish Colleen's brave girl. "She said I could tell her anything."

Irish Colleen let her sigh go. "Elizabeth, what have we talked about?"

"That... that adults think they want to help, but adults don't understand our world."

Irish Colleen finished the braid and pulled Elizabeth around. "Mrs. Larsen has been very good to you. She's a good teacher. A good woman, godly. But you told her something today that had her very concerned. And now you need to tell me."

"I can't." Elizabeth pointed her chin at the far wall, but Irish Colleen had it in her hands and pulled it back.

"Yes, you can. Unlike Mrs. Larsen, who means well but can't understand, I won't punish you. Not for this. Tell me, Elizabeth."

"I *can't*."

"You can't, or you won't?"

"Mama, I can't, don't ask me. Don't!"

"Does this have to do with what you said about Charles earlier?"

"No." Elizabeth wiped at her eyes and paused in mid-gesture. "Maybe. I don't know! It's not clear. It's never clear when I need it to be, Mama. It's just jumbles and swirls and my head is full to bursting with them." She smashed her palms against her temples in fitful demonstration.

The temperature in the room dropped. All the hair on Irish Colleen's arms stood at attention. It was happening again, like it did when August died, but she had to know. She had to hear, because Colleen Brady Deschanel had never been much for surprises, especially the very bad ones.

She pulled her daughter's tear-drenched cheeks into her palms and forced Elizabeth to confront the moment at hand. "Elizabeth, tell me. Whatever it is, no matter how bad. We don't hide from things in this house."

Elizabeth sucked in her bottom lip. Snot and tears slid over Irish Colleen's hands, but she didn't drop them. "It's not clear..."

"Tell me anyway."

"One of us..." Elizabeth pressed her hands to her eyes and nose and wiped them. Her gaze traveled briefly to the window and the storm outside. Where did the rain come from? "One of us, one of the seven, is going to die at the end of the year and I don't think we can stop it, Mama."

Who? Irish Colleen almost asked.

As if it mattered.

As if the loss of any of her babies would ever, ever be a loss she could bear.

Irish Colleen didn't consciously drop her hands from the face of her daughter, nor did she mean to back away and then rise, pressing her slippers into one step after another, toward the door, away from the monstrous proclamations of a child she loved with all her heart but did not know how to protect.

Elizabeth's sobs pierced Irish Colleen's heart from the hallway as she clicked the door closed and stepped into the swash of moonlight that no longer seemed a sign from God, but a warning from beyond.

CHAPTER 1

The Altruist and the Adherent

Madeline Deschanel scribbled furiously in the lines and margins of the last gift her father gave her before he died: a diary. It was a bulky book with a bloated plastic cover bubbling up off the cardboard with peeling pink and blue elephants. When she'd opened it on her eighth birthday, she'd gaped at it, confused, until her father shyly explained he got the idea from the way Madeline excitedly watched the elephants at Audubon Zoo.

"August, I told you she doesn't really like elephants," her mother chastised under her breath, as she sorted through the rest of the gifts. She tossed them in neat piles as if birthdays were a chore and not a blessing.

"Daddy was right, I love elephants," Madeline lied and wrapped her arms around her father's shoulders, because already at eight she understood all men, even one as confident and assuming as August Deschanel, needed validation. Even when you had to be dishonest in the offering.

Madeline didn't use the diary then. In truth, she had no desire to catalogue her thoughts, which were a plaguing nuisance and always had been. What benefit could possibly be had by reliving them? No, she didn't pick it up for many years, and when she finally did, the catalyst was the original giver of the gift, her father.

The fight Madeline had with her mother on her sixteenth birthday wasn't unusual—the fighting part anyway; they didn't need an occasion for that—but her mother's choice to invoke her dead husband was a new and pointed dagger that hit precisely where she intended.

"The drama in your life is going to kill you," Irish Colleen harped, after the party came to an abrupt halt with Madeline's mention of going to a war protest at Louis Armstrong Park. She couldn't understand how her mother had refused her this. It was the perfect compromise. It wasn't a trip to Washington, or California. She could be a part of something without even leaving their city, and now she suspected her mother was less concerned with whether or not Madeline wanted to protest, and more with controlling her and turning her into the perfect little daughter.

"It isn't drama, Mother. People in the world are suffering, while we stuff our faces with roast and duck in our antebellum mansion, with our pretty gardens and old money."

"Says the young woman who has never known real hardship. Has never had to wonder where her next meal would come from," her mother had said, without looking at her, her attention instead divided between minimizing her daughter's plight and tidying up the dining room. She ran a rag over the old wood, catching some rogue icing. Outside, a hearse led a line of Benzes and Cadillacs toward Lafayette Cemetery No. 1; both a byproduct of living so close to the cemetery, and, as far as Madeline was concerned, a prophetic reminder of what life was like at Oak Haven under her mother's rule.

Madeline had wedged herself between her mother and the messy table. "I'm not ignorant to the privilege I've had, Mother. Not like Charles, who runs around snorting cocaine and screwing half of New Orleans while the rest of the world suffers. I'm smart enough to understand I have a responsibility to use my privilege to help the world."

"A smart person knows they can't solve the world's problems and instead focuses on their own." Irish Colleen continued to wipe down the tables with the same disinterested look. She had never taken any of it seriously. Not Madeline's desperate emotions and not the fact the world burned while they lived a life of luxury. Of all people, Irish Colleen should have been the one to grasp it. She'd been a river rat who spent half her youth homeless, and the other half searching for the opportunity that would pull her out of a life devoid of hope.

"You don't understand!" Madeline cried, cake sliding from her plate in one hand, a new Janis Joplin record slipping from the other. "I'm an empath, Mom. I *feel* things. I didn't ask for this. I didn't ask to feel every single death in Vietnam, or to mourn Dr. King and Robert Kennedy like I mourned Dad. You don't know how it feels to be me, so don't you dare act like it's nothing. Dad would have understood!"

"Your father." Irish Colleen's voice shook. Her fists went white at her sides, the mess forgotten. Now she was paying attention. "You didn't ask for this? Well, *I* didn't ask for this either, Madeline! I didn't ask for my husband to lie to me about who he was, marry me, and then leave me with seven children who are as strange and unusual as him!"

Madeline felt the wrath emanate from her mother in violent waves. Even a normal person could have felt this, it was so potent, but as an empath, she absorbed it straight into herself, into the tiny pores, a direct injection to her marrow, attaching to her soul.

She dropped her cake and her record, and ran straight to her room. Instinct carried her to the shoebox in her closet filled with things long-forgotten, and she pulled out the ugly diary, crushed it to her chest shaking from sobs, deciding then and there that her father would want her to find an outlet for all the emotion trapped inside her.

Now, almost two years later, she had run out of paper, so she wrote smaller and into the margins, entries wrapping in spirals and into the four corners. She would continue this until there wasn't a single white space left. She didn't look forward to that day. If she was someone else, she would just buy another journal, but Madeline wasn't someone else. Every drop of ink on this page kept her father alive in her heart. Kept her from completely losing her mind, once and for all.

The words flowed from her heart to the liberating sound of Crosby, Stills, & Nash floating off her record player. Madeline closed her eyes and dropped a tab of LSD on her tongue. She swayed to the music and lifted her pen.

Mike Wallace said on 60 Minutes that Nixon has over a half-million of our boys in Vietnam now, when the war should have ended last year. It should have never started! Big things are happening in Washington, D.C. and I have to get there and be with people like me, who are burning for change and can't sit around waiting for it.

We must *lower the voting age to eighteen. We have to get these warmongers out of our highest offices.*

I don't care what Mom says anymore. She'll never have to send her own sons off to war. She didn't understand why Woodstock was so important. She doesn't understand how music can change things! What hurts the most is she doesn't even try to understand me. She thinks we're all freaks. Maybe we are.

Madeline shook her cramping hand. The tiny lettering was a challenge, but she wasn't ready to be done with this journal, and she had to preserve the remaining space. She wouldn't be done with this journal until she was free of New Orleans and her mother.

She almost fell off her bed when her door opened. She clutched her chest. "Augustus! I almost flipped my wig, you dope."

Her older brother grinned. A flush hit his soft, round cheeks. "You know I don't understand half of what you say, Maddy."

"So, it's my fault you're such a drag?"

Augustus plopped next to her on the bed and threw a shoulder at her. He caught her before she fell. "I'm trying to make something of my life. I don't have time to be hip."

"And I'm trying to make something of the *world*."

"I know." He rubbed the top of her head, mussing her wavy hair. "You will. When you're eighteen."

He did know. Or, tried to. He was the only one who tried, and the irony that her most serious, most focused sibling was the only one who took the time to understand her was not lost on Madeline.

She rolled her eyes. "You assume I'll last that long under Comrade Mom."

"You have less than a year to go. If you don't have the fortitude to survive a few more months in the house you grew up in, how are you going to find the patience and grit to effect change in the world?"

Madeline groaned. "I hate Augustus logic."

"That's not true. You said you look up to me."

"You're the lunatic who still lives here."

Augustus folded his hands in his lap. "It's easier to focus when I don't have to worry about putting a roof over my head."

"You're a Deschanel, you dope. You'll *never* have to worry about putting a roof over your head." She couldn't hide the venom, which wasn't directed at him at all, and she hoped he knew that.

"I just want to get through business school so I can start my company. Why would I add complications I don't need? I don't care whether Mom is strict or doesn't understand us. Not like you do."

"You *should* care," she accused. "It's part of who you are."

"It isn't all of who we are," he said patiently. "Besides, I also stay for you."

Madeline leaned into her brother. The musky scent of his oaky aftershave, his only personal indulgence, evoked a sensation of security she couldn't find in any other way in this wretched mansion. With Augustus, she was safe. She may chide him for staying, but he was the only reason she hadn't fled herself.

"I just wanted to see how you were doing," he went on. "I heard things got hairy with Mom when I came in from class. Are you okay?"

Madeline's head spun. The acid had kicked in, and the posters on her wall danced before her eyes. Jimi Hendrix twitched in a rousing guitar solo as the rainbow waves gyrated in chorus. Sweat poured down his strained face, and then he looked up and winked at her. She burst into laughter.

Augustus placed his hand on her jaw and turned her head. "Are you high?"

Her grin spread far enough across her face to make her teeth ache. "If I am?"

He shook his head in disgust but said nothing more about it. He never had and never would. In these ways, he showed he cared, both by noticing and then by ultimately not berating her. "So, are you? Okay?"

"I'll be a lot better when Mom stops treating us like dogs she wants to come to heel."

"She's raising seven children by herself. Have you ever stopped to consider how easily you empathize with the soldiers in Vietnam, when you find it so hard to understand our own mother's pain?"

Madeline punched his shoulder. Her fist slid off the soft polyester of his sweater and bent in a strange position. She shook the pain away. "Stop defending her! Whose side are you on?"

"There are two sides to everything, Maddy. The world is easier when you accept that."

Her eyes rolled back into her head and she flopped back onto her pillow.

"And I'm always on your side," her brother said, low enough she could barely hear him over the music. "You know that."

Madeline rocked back into a seated position and rested her face in Augustus' shoulder blades. "And you know if you wake up one day and I'm not here, it isn't because you weren't on my side."

"You promised me you'd finish high school."

"I promised I would *try.*"

Augustus spun around. "Sounds like you've made up your mind."

"What, you gonna go fink to Mom?"

"Stop accusing me of unfair things." Rather than angry, he sounded hurt.

Madeline, contrite, wrapped her arms around his neck and squeezed. "You're right. I'm sorry, Aggie. You're the very best brother in the wide world. I wouldn't have lasted this long without you." She peppered his cheeks with manic kisses.

Augustus grunted, but his stiffness melted away. He squeezed her once, then peeled her off. "Okay, okay. I need to study."

She pointed her thumb down and made a disgusted sound with her lips. "You do that, Aggie, and I'll just be in here making a plan to end the Cold War and bring our boys home from 'Nam."

Her brother—her only ally in this world—smiled before disappearing into the hallway.

It was true that Augustus was the only reason she hadn't run far, far away from New Orleans years ago. He protected her, but it was so much more than that. He didn't look at Madeline and wish she were someone else, someone better. Someone more grounded, like him, or perfect Colleen. When she told him she meant to be a part of ending the war, his only ask was she finish school.

She was trying. For him.

But every day under this roof, with a mother who looked at her more like a disappointment than a daughter, and a life she could hardly stand to look upon without a twisted self-loathing that the rest of the world didn't have such luxuries, tested her fortitude for the task.

Madeline rolled over on her side and lifted the stylus on the record player. She was done with Crosby, Stills, and Nash for now. She slipped out James Taylor's "Sweet Baby James."

Leaning back against her pile of plush pillows, Madeline let the soft melodies carry her into the best part of her trip.

COLLEEN SCRIBBLED FURIOUS NOTES INTO THE SPIRAL book resting precisely parallel to her physics textbook. Her messy shorthand looked like nonsensical loops and spirals to others, but she could decipher every word. She first learned this skill as a method for keeping up with her frenetic mind, which moved at the speed of tomorrow. Now, she saw it as an edge to her future in medical school, where the incomprehensible scrawl would become part of the science.

Only a month remained until finals, and then summer, and then... college. Colleen felt in her soul that she had been preparing for college since kindergarten, and many of her teachers had expressed similar sentiments about her, though couched in the form of concern. *When her friends are playing at recess, Colleen hides in the library.* Of course, Colleen's mother, Irish Colleen, always came back with the expected incredulous response. *You're calling me in because Colleen is* too *good of a student? Is that right?*

Irish Colleen never went to college herself. She had given up halfway through high school to first take care of her mother, and then later, was a hospice caregiver for the first wife of August Deschanel, Eliza, in her final months of life. August had loved Eliza, and she gave him everything he could ever want in the form of love, but Eliza was unable to give him what he needed, and that was children. Until he had an heir, the family would be in nervous limbo. Heartbroken but resolved, August turned right around and married Irish Colleen, and then the rest—seven live children, a handful of miscarriages, a marriage of mostly convenience but occasionally love —was history.

But Irish Colleen was determined her children would benefit from the vast Deschanel fortune left to them by their late father and pushed them all into their studies whether the shoe fit or not. As it happened, the shoe only fit Colleen and Augustus, but Irish Colleen pushed each of the seven nonetheless, determined every one of her children would have the life she didn't, never wondering if her expectations matched their desires.

The Deschanel name alone guaranteed each of them a spot at any of the New Orleans private universities. This was the only reason Charles found his way to university at all. Colleen was determined to not only prove herself worthy upon arrival, but every moment thereafter. She was especially conscious her name would open doors for the rest of her life, and she would have no one saying she didn't deserve to step through them.

"I'm so *tired* of The Doors," Carolina whined. Rory stretched the record over both their heads, out of her reach. She made tiny grunting sounds as she leaped for it.

Colleen fell out of her daze. She'd completely forgotten her two best friends were even there. This happened all the time, and she wondered if they knew. "How about no music?"

Rory pivoted through them both, using the bed as leverage, and deftly landed on his feet in front of the record player. "You know you dig it." He placed the record on the player and settled the needle on the track. He closed his eyes and let his head feel the music as the first notes of "Hello, I Love You" flowed through the room.

"Ugh," Carolina simpered, but she giggled as Rory offered both hands and pulled her to the floor. He gyrated into The Twist and she matched him move for move, squealing in joy despite her declared loathing of The Doors.

Rory hooted and spun Carolina in circles around the shag carpet, over and over until she wobbled from the dizziness, but his eyes stayed on Colleen alone. He curled the corner of his mouth in a smile that took them both out of the moment.

Colleen smiled back, then dropped her eyes back to her studies. She sometimes felt the pull to be as cool and carefree as beautiful Carolina with her thick gold headbands and sizzler skirts, dancing around a bedroom on the eve of the rest of her life. To drop all her worries into her bedside drawer and abandon herself to the moment, even provisionally. Surely there was no harm in fleeting episodes of fun. No harm in letting it all go from time to time.

But Colleen felt the substance of who she was had always tightly coiled itself within her, and unraveling this, even a little, would risk a loss of control she wasn't prepared to handle.

When the song ended, Carolina sighed and flopped back on the bed, flushed. She fanned herself like she'd just run a marathon. "*Now,* can we listen to something else?"

Rory crossed his arms. "I have a better idea."

"You have my rapt attention," Carolina coquetted.

Rory looked at Colleen. "What would it take to convince you

going to the skating rink with us is a better idea than studying for a test you have zero chance of not acing?"

Colleen frowned. "Rory Sullivan, it's easy for you to say when you've had a spot awaiting you at Sullivan & Associates since before your birth."

"As if a Deschanel couldn't be anything in the world," Carolina teased with a dramatic eye roll. She tugged at her headband, which had come loose in their dance party.

Rory clutched his chest feigning offense. "You cut me, Leena, cut me deep. I take my studies seriously."

Colleen let her expression travel between her two friends speaking for her.

"I do!" he protested. "I'll still have to pass the bar exam one day, you know."

"I'm relatively certain several Sullivans required multiple retakes. This doesn't inspire confidence."

"They eventually passed."

Colleen pressed her spiral notebook into the textbook, resting her hand there as well to hold her spot. "You two go. Have fun. I'll catch up later when I finish," she lied.

Carolina leaned over Colleen's vanity table, coiffing her hair back into place. She bounced up. "You better come!" she exclaimed. She squeezed Rory's arm and leaned in. "I need to use the little girls' room. Meet you in the car, sport?"

He nodded and blew her an emphatic kiss, which she nearly tripped catching as she fell into the hall.

Rory returned his focus to Colleen. "I know you're not really going to show up later."

"Yeah." Colleen tried to look ashamed. She felt ashamed, but not enough to cause her to change what drove her fundamentally toward the future she desired for herself. Would Rory be there with her in one year? Five? It hurt a little to think of his absence, but she doubted it. No one really took high school with them when they left, unless they failed to move on. "But you have fun with Carolina. She digs you."

Rory shoved his hands in the pockets of his burnt orange trousers, which were utterly ridiculous, and even unfashionable. Colleen knew that. "It isn't like that."

Colleen chuckled. "It could be, with very little effort on your part."

He shook his head. "No. You don't understand."

Colleen's heartbeat escalated as his words hung between them. *Some things are better left never addressed.*

Rory reached a hand forward and pushed her unruly bangs aside. His smile, always present, but always different to fit the occasion, was more serious than usual, and Colleen was suddenly afraid.

A blaring horn caused them both to jump back. "I guess I better split. Can't keep the princess waiting. Keep it real, Leena." He stopped in the doorway. "And if you really wanna blow my mind, show up later in spite of yourself. You'll have fun. I'll make sure of it."

Colleen pressed her hands to her cheeks, which were burning hot, so hot she was certain he could see it and was relieved when he finally disappeared. She smiled into her notebook.

"He digs you so hard it makes me wanna gag," Evangeline declared from the hallway. She sauntered into the room, uninvited, her wild hair taking up all the available real estate around her head. Colleen set her expression and pressed her hands to the crazy mane.

"He does not," Colleen said, less because she believed it and more because she had no desire to entertain the idea at all.

"He's going to ask you to prom," Evangeline went on, with the confidence of someone who knows more than they should. "Will you say yes?"

"He is not. And what would you know about it?"

"Oh, he is. He told Chelsea, who told Roger, who told me."

"I doubt he'd tell his *sister* anything of the sort. And he would have asked already if he was going to. There's hardly time to get a dress." Colleen shook her head. "In any case, you're wrong. He's not going to ask, and I'm not planning to go, anyway."

"You spend all your time with him." The words sounded less an observation than an accusation.

"I spend all my time studying."

Evangeline wasn't buying it. "He's always in your room."

"So is Carolina, and she isn't asking me to prom."

"You're wrong. He's in love with you, and he's going to ask."

Colleen set her books aside. There was only one reason she could come up with that Evangeline would press this hard. "I know we haven't spent much time together lately, Evie. College is so close, and I don't want to mess anything up."

Evangeline rolled her head and waved her hand. "As if I don't have better things to do, anyway. Like dissecting the neighborhood cats and blowing up barns with homemade explosives. You know, genius things."

Colleen pulled her close. Evangeline stiffened and then curled into her sister.

"It's only going to get worse when you go to college," Evangeline said. Her voice was strained at the hint of vulnerability she was always so loath to display.

"I promise it won't."

"I hope you know that continuously promising things you can't deliver is the sign of a personality disorder."

Colleen pushed her forward and settled Evangeline between her legs so she was behind her. "I'm glad psychology class isn't wasted on you. Now sit still. I'll get this hair into braids if it's the last thing I do."

"Maybe Paul will ask you to prom, now that he's not a Beatle anymore," Evangeline mused. "Or maybe you'll just go with Rory."

"Don't be silly. You know I prefer Ringo."

"Colleen, *no one* prefers Ringo."

COLLEEN DID NOT BLOW RORY'S MIND THAT NIGHT. SHE had other plans, ones she could not explain adequately to anyone who wasn't part of their unusual family. Rory and Carolina knew she had family obligations some evenings, but the extent of them was a secret Colleen kept close to her heart.

She navigated the endless hallways of The Gardens. When the mansion had been built, in the mid-nineteenth century, the Deschanels intended it as a home capable of housing the entire family. Today, the megalith Greek Revival spanned nearly an entire city block all on its own, and no matter how many times Colleen had been there, it always left her with the dizzying sensation she was navigating a maze with the propensity to change directions on a whim. One of her cousins told her they were quite certain the location of the bathrooms had altered more than once.

She paused outside the heavy oaken doors, taking in the familiar scent of very old wood and ancient secrets. Beyond, her fellow Deschanel Magi Collective Council peers awaited. The august body of family senators that used to rule the Council had died off, and today's Council was much younger and more modern. Colleen, at eighteen, wasn't even the youngest. Her cousin Kitty Guidry was two years her junior.

The Council of seven ruled over the Collective, making decisions for the family that could not be spoken of in public or the exposure of daylight. They often met at the chime of the witching hour, in a cavernous room absent of natural light, brightened only by sconces lining the paneled walls. It smelled permanently of the ancients.

Colleen opened the door. Her peers were already there, and she took her usual seat. They all gathered at the near end of the table that stretched far enough into the dim room that the end could not be seen without taking a candle into the darkness.

Eugenia and Cassius gathered around the magistrate, helping her settle into her seat. At ninety-two, Ophelia Deschanel's gnarled, hunched form struggled to find bearing, but her mind was sharper than the rest of them combined.

"Yes, yes, that will be enough, thank you." Ophelia's scratched voice dismissed them, and they dutifully fell into their own seats.

Ophelia folded her heavily wrinkled hands. A slight but permanent tremor rocked her, but she seemed unbothered by this, or by any of her limitations. Yellow teeth appeared behind her crooked smile. "Shall we begin with our vows, then." It was not a question.

She didn't attempt to stand again. Instead, she linked her hands with Eugenia to her right and Kitty to her left, and the rest of the Council followed suit. "In power, obligation."

"In power, obligation," repeated the other six.

"In obligation, commitment." She paused for the echo. "In commitment, solidarity." Another pause for the group to reprise. "In solidarity, enlightenment."

"And lastly," finished Ophelia, "the Council also lives under governance, through enlightenment."

"Through governance, enlightenment," Colleen recited back, with her cousins, in a room filled with centuries of secrets and yet another side of her life that would always be shut away from the one she shared with her friends in the world beyond.

"First order of business," Ophelia began. "The solar eclipse is next week. We have reports from Sweden that we should be monitoring for unusual supernatural activity. Our archives have stories from the 1851 eclipse that confirm we may be in for a very interesting celestial event, my dearests."

Pansy clapped her hands together in delight. "Groovy."

"What sorts of stories?" asked Cassius. Beside him, Pierce nodded, confirming he shared the question.

"The usual madness we see when seasons change," Ophelia replied. Her small body shook as a cough took over. Kitty's hand hovered in mid-air as she decided whether to intervene. She dropped it when Ophelia wiped her hand across her mouth and continued. "Animals running off or acting out of character. Aggression, fear, or even the opposite, at times. Ordinarily docile husbands raising hands against wives, or even the reverse, women taking the lives of their men and later claiming no memory of the act. Libidos running wild, people abandoning their senses. Nothing too unexpected."

Pierce blinked a few times. "Orgies and murder... why, I never..."

"You don't really believe these reports?" Eugenia added.

Ophelia's smile was lazy, knowing.

Colleen remembered that her older brother, Charles, had been invited to an eclipse party at the Weatherly estate. "Should we be concerned, Aunt Ophelia?"

"The scientists say no," Ophelia said carefully. She stretched her bony fingers. A face that had seen many, many things over the course of a very long lifetime looked directly at Colleen. "But science and magic play together in ways science doesn't understand and never will. We know any time the moon, sun, or stars act outside of the usual, it changes things within a man, or a woman if you will, that science can't explain and magic doesn't need to. Much like a full moon or a change in the tides, I expect yes, the darkening of the sun will bring out the unusual in many, and scientists will spend years explaining it away. But we will know."

Ophelia slowly looked around the room. "That's why we are here. Because we know."

CHAPTER 2
Fortunate Son

Charles Deschanel confidently strolled through the tropical garden of Dan Weatherly's property like no one had more right to be there. The young men and women gathered for the party paused in mid-conversation when he passed by them. Would he stop? Say hello? Share a bump of coke? Charles threw out peace signs and grins with calculated intention, well aware every choice he made would be examined later. Every gesture would be interpreted and re-interpreted, and hearts would soar or break based on their conclusions. Breaths were held until he moved on, but everyone resumed their conversations and fun, feeling a little cooler now that the playboy of New Orleans was on the scene.

His best friend, Colin Sullivan, winced as a cascade of water shot from the pool when they walked by. "Sorry! I forgot to call cannonball!" a girl in a green string bikini yelled from the center. She rolled her head back to receive the arcing water from a set of double fountains shaped like fish heads. Colin waved back, but the look of discomfort he'd worn since they stepped out of Charles' Trans Am intensified.

"I don't know how I let you talk me into coming."

"If you stopped being a square, the sun would stop circling the moon," Charles accused with a tousle of his friend's neatly combed hair. "But it doesn't mean I'll stop trying."

"But the sun doesn—"

"Come on, let's hydrate," Charles declared and sauntered away from the pool, in the direction of the back porch. A butler held aloft a silver tray of champagne, and Charles snapped up the last two before another nearby nobody could take them. "Here, drink. It will help you chill."

Colin accepted the fluted glass with a wince of distaste. He sipped through pursed lips, but Charles didn't see the liquid level go down at all. "Do you think they have water?"

"You're drinking Dom Perignon and you're asking about water?"

"It's hardly ten in the morning, Charles."

"They're drinking in Paris, so why shouldn't we?"

From the vantage point of the porch, Charles surveyed the whole backyard, from the lush garden of lantana and irises, to the kidney-shaped pool, to the guesthouse tucked into the rear corners, flanked by thorny bougainvillea and all colors of roses. Butterflies fluttered through the hazy afternoon, landing on all manner of surfaces. Cicadas buzzed, keeping tune to the persistent background hum of their world. But Charles paid no mind to the inherent liveliness of their subtropical world. He had eyes only for the human inhabitants.

He'd been performing this subconscious act since his eyes fell on the first girl at the party, assessing. Was she the one? No. It was rarely ever the first one he saw. He almost never got that lucky. He'd already bagged many of them, though never more than once or twice, and never in succession. He couldn't be seen as tied down, or unavailable, though there were some women, certain types, who flocked to that, too, so sometimes it worked in his favor.

Then there were the ones he wouldn't touch if the world was ending. He was enough of a gentleman not to say this to their faces, but he found other ways for the information to reach them. He found it better to avoid uncomfortable moments by heading them off with well-spread gossip.

Between these two types of women enjoying the Weatherly party—at most parties in New Orleans now—this didn't leave Charles with many options. Dan had promised fresh meat at his eclipse bash, for which invitations were coveted. Only the wealthy elite, the old money crowd, were welcome, though these rules applied mainly to the men, and not at all to the host, who was only second generation self-made department store wealth, but rich enough that this only mattered in very certain circumstances.

As for the ladies, a beautiful woman was a beautiful woman, and allowing the finest to enter only enhanced the worthiness of the event.

No one even cared about the eclipse, but an excuse to party wasn't taken for granted.

Charles scanned. Let his eyes fall over each person, long enough only to make his usual assessment. The wilting heat melted the ice in his drink and added a blanket of haze to the day, affecting his vision. Bikinis ran together into a mess of color, a rainbow of sexual pleasure. They were all the same, all of them. Blonde. Brunette. Redhead. Rinse. Repeat. He couldn't even be sure if he'd had some of them. The women in their circle had begun to take on the same expensive smile, shrill laugh, perfectly sculpted body. They enjoyed the same range of drugs, jived to the same music, and went home with the same men. Droll. Droll. Droll.

"I don't like this, Charles."

"You mentioned that already." Charles pulled a large cross necklace from out of his collared shirt. The pendant separated in two, revealing a small silver spoon. He rotated to the side and took a quick bump. Sniffed. Winced. "Want one?"

"Do I need to answer that?"

Charles looped his arm around Colin's shoulders. A cigarette bobbed from his mouth as he gestured around with his free hand. "Look around you. Everyone is stoned, drunk, or flying higher than the sky. Do you see any of them complaining?"

"*Everyone else is doing it,* is a low argument, even for you."

Charles closed his eyes and moved his head to the music. The cocaine hit him fast and hard, but he was ready for another bump. He released a long stream of smoke out of his nose, enjoying the burn. "You're missing my point, buddy. There's not an unhappy person here, because they're feeling the flow. Who's the odd man out?"

"What I see," Colin said, hugging his polo shirt tighter around him, "is a bunch of trust fund elites whose parents will bail them out of whatever trouble they get in today."

"You're not a lawyer yet, Colin. Maybe try having some fun before you're stuck pushing papers and bailing these trust fund elites out of their trouble." Charles blew his smoke toward the sky. He regarded the dying embers at the tip of his butt, pressed between his thumb and forefinger. Pulling one last drag, he flicked it off into the bushes.

"Jesus, Charles, are you trying to start a fire?"

"It's copacetic, brother," Charles answered, though his attention had shifted back to scanning the partygoers for the woman he would pleasure—or more likely, would pleasure him—before the sun disappeared.

THE WORLD AROUND THEM BEGAN TO DIM SHORTLY before eleven.

Charles didn't notice it at first. The women clinging from each of his arms giggled and demurred, blocking out the conversation around him. Four—or was it six? Or nine?—glasses of champagne later, he eventually grabbed the bottle and doused it over one of the girls paying court to him, then licked the expensive alcohol from her toned flesh to the cheers of nearby sycophants. Cheers turned to howls when he pushed her bikini bottom aside and finished there. He was so high he couldn't discern between the flavor of her nectar and that of the champagne, but only one would force him to rinse his mouth later.

What kind of woman would let you do that to her in front of an audience? Charles heard Colin's voice in his head only. He vaguely recalled his friend had left in disgust at some indistinct point, possibly right after Charles had run out of cocaine and had to cozy up to this new group to obtain more.

Someone yelled for more champagne. Charles pulled himself up off his knees and drew the same girl he'd just finished on into a deep kiss, all tongue, hoping to transfer some of her juices back to her and avoid terrible breath later. High fives flew over his head, which spun just enough for him to wonder if what he needed was more drugs, or fewer.

Charles wiped his hand across his mouth. Around him, the party had evolved... or devolved, depending on the perspective. He spotted Dan Weatherly lying on a lawn chair being ridden by some blonde. Dan, the host, the only man here *not* old money, but his parties were so legend no one cared. Dan's eyes were closed, and Charles couldn't tell if he had passed out or was caught in the ecstasy. The other lawn chairs beheld similar spectacles, a veritable orgy in perfect synchronization. Just beyond them, a group of partiers waved their hands in front of them, playing with acid tracers only they could see. He turned his head again, and this time lost footing and fell into a guy holding the empty Dom Perignon bottle like a trophy. He righted Charles and dusted off something imaginary from his shorts. Near the guesthouse, under a break in the canopy of oaks, others played with cardboard boxes, positioning them toward the sun, which had not grown dark so much as... subdued, like someone had thrown a filter over it, or hit the dimmer switch.

Nails scratched his cheek. One of his groupies pulled his face down to her breasts, but he wasn't in the mood, and she didn't do anything for him, except... she was offering him something else altogether. She'd poured a haphazard line across the perfect milky arc popping from her bikini top. Charles buried his face and sucked in through his nose so hard his head spun for a moment. She moaned like a woman in the throes of orgasm.

"There's more where that came from," she cooed, and Charles decided then and there that it didn't matter if he was into her, because she had something he wanted even more than sex.

CHARLES DIDN'T REMEMBER THE PRECISE MOMENT HE blacked out, but when he awoke, he was looking up at the sky. He blinked, once and then again, to bring it into focus, but the haze that stole the brightness from the sky wouldn't dissipate. He pressed his eyes closed for longer this time, and when he opened them, he was convinced he was going blind.

He whipped his head around to see if others were experiencing this, but bodies piled over the lawn, on chairs, around the pool, sleeping off their high. A few made sluggish attempts at some sexual act or another, thrusting momentarily before falling into a lapse, but none looked alert, looked up, looked toward the sky, where the world was ending.

Pleasure rippled through him and he realized the girl from earlier, the cocaine queen, had her fingers pressed into his chest as she bounced on his cock with a frenetic enthusiasm that didn't match the subdued world around them.

"You like that, Daddy? You like that?" The question repeated, over and over, and she didn't wait for an answer. The words came from her like a broken record that knew nothing but the jilted refrain.

Charles floated in and out of consciousness to the sounds of the Stones blaring over the porch speakers. The world went from dim to dark, dark to dim. The cocaine queen either didn't notice or didn't mind his disconnect from her earnest work, for she continued with zeal.

Her droning questions faded from his ears, though her lips continued to press the words into existence. Charles rolled his head to the side. Something was all wrong, all wrong. The sun... it was there, but it was... something was...

Charles leaned over the side of the chair and threw up.

The cocaine queen paused long enough to ask if he was okay, and a light nod was enough for her to continue her emphatic ministrations. Charles wondered briefly at her dedication, for his cock was half-limp and he hadn't so much as given her a word of encouragement.

"Gimme Shelter" rippled through the remains of the party, bouncing off the trees, the music, like everyone, everyone but Charles, blissfully unaware that the sun was slowly disappearing from the world, and that without the sun, there could be no life.

"Shut it off, someone shut off the fucking music!" he cried, not sure why this, of all things, was so important.

"I'll make it better, Daddy, let me make it better," the cocaine queen soothed, and Charles left the world again for a few moments.

WHEN HE AWOKE THIS TIME, THE COCAINE QUEEN HAD her lips wrapped around his cock. He tried to sit forward, to say something, but the dizziness swept him back.

"You have whiskey dick, Daddy, but I can fix it," she explained, as if they were talking about making groceries.

"I didn't drink whiskey," he mumbled, and a mouthful of old vomit sent a new wave of sickness over him. On his tongue rested the remnants of his earlier decisions, and none of it blended well together, which was no surprise, for none of his decisions ever did. He closed his eyes, but this didn't help, not when the world outside was so *dim* and nothing would ever be the same again.

Mercifully, someone had turned off the music at some point, but this revealed a new horror.

Complete, utter, terrifying silence.

The Garden District was a world alive at every clematis tendril, every magnolia bloom. From the rustling of exotic flora to the insistent, grating songs of the bees and cicadas, it was a world abuzz, always, at all times of the day.

Except it wasn't. He heard not a whisper of a shifting vine. Not even a distant buzz of the cicadas, or the chirp of a rogue katydid.

From the corner of his eye, he noted Dan's dog pacing an anxious, repeating semi-circle through the lawn.

His mother said something once. Something inconsequential at the time, but now seemed to be the only words that mattered. *That's when the world will end, when the cicadas stop singing.*

The air screamed with the absence of sound. It ricocheted through his head, taunting him, demanding of him if *this* is how he saw his final moments on the Earth.

Cocaine queen crawled back atop him. Her sweaty legs wrapped around him.

Someone—maybe his mother, maybe the anchorman on Channel 7 News—had said not to stare at the sun during the eclipse, but nothing could have pulled his eyes away now. Even with the dimness turned down around him, the sun was still excruciatingly bright, and this juxtapose confused him even more than how he was somehow the only one aware they were on the verge of the world ending.

"It's so... beautiful," he whispered, and a new peace washed over him. He would see his father again, and there was nothing he had ever wished for more.

Charles was so disconnected from the moment at hand that the shock of orgasm rocking through his body caused him to cry out, breaking a slash through the silence blanketing the dark and dying world.

BRIGHTNESS RETURNED TO THE SKY.

The cicadas hummed to life.

The cocaine queen adjusted her bikini bottoms into place. Her ass jiggled as she snapped the stretchy fabric against her flesh.

She leaned down and tucked his cock into his boxer shorts with a soft pat, almost motherly.

He squinted up at her, her soft baby cheeks, the strange innocence he hadn't noticed earlier. "How old are you, cocaine queen?"

"Shelly," she said with a frown he didn't feel he'd earned from someone he'd only met an hour or so ago. "We had fun, didn't we, Daddy?"

"I'm not your daddy."

She dropped her arms on either side of him. She smelled of sweat and expensive champagne. His stomach turned. "Fourteen, Daddy. But I fuck like I'm twenty."

Charles rolled to the side and released the rest of the morning into the flagstones.

Charles lost a few more hours between Shelly's departure and the moment he stumbled through the front door of Oak Haven.

His brother, Augustus, headed him off before he'd even made it into the foyer. "Mama is on a warpath. Where the hell have you been?"

Charles smacked his mouth, which was still a smorgasbord of all the day's indiscretions. "I saw… I saw the most glorious thing." He slapped his hands over his brother's arms. "The world almost ended today, and then it didn't. We're still here, brother. God is good."

Augustus sighed. "We *all* saw it. The world wasn't ending. Not over an eclipse anyway." He pulled Charles to the side. "The Dean of Tulane called about you."

"Yeah? Anything good?"

"You know it wasn't." Augustus looked around, tense. "It never is."

"What does it matter? What does any of it matter?"

"It's your future!"

"Our future is anything we want it to be, Augustus. Why do you kill yourself studying? You'll never have to work a day in your life. Neither will I."

Augustus narrowed his eyes. "That's not me. Maybe you, but not me."

"Charles August Deschanel!" cried the powerful voice of Irish

Colleen. Her heavy footsteps echoed across the cypress. "Where the devil have you been?"

Augustus raised his eyebrows and faded into the hallway.

"I was at Dan's for the eclipse." That wasn't her question. It never really was. When she asked where he'd been, she was searching for something deeper, perhaps answers as to why he was such a massive disappointment in her eyes.

Irish Colleen snaked her tiny hands up and rotated his face back and forth. She pulled it down then and inspected his eyes. "You're high." She moved on to frenetic sniffing. "And you smell like... cigarettes and booze." Her mouth curled in disgust. "And worse."

"I'm home for dinner," came his weak return. He braced himself for the slap and was not disappointed.

"Do you know how much money we've donated to Tulane? Do you have any idea how much work it has been to keep you in school?"

"They'll get over it," Charles said. He winced again, but this time she only stood before him, fuming. He preferred her violent reactions. They made him angrier, too, which diluted her disappointment.

"I ask only *one* thing of you. One! I ask that you go to your college classes, and not do anything dumb enough to get yourself kicked out before you can graduate."

"Technically, that's two things."

Irish Colleen shook her tiny fist. "Most mothers don't have to ask their sons *not to get kicked out of school,* but here we are, Charles. Thank God your father isn't here to see this. He would be so ashamed."

"Father would have known college is pointless for me. I'm the heir to the greatest dynasty in Louisiana. I'll never have to work a day in my life," Charles returned, though even as the words flowed, he felt the lie in them. August Deschanel wouldn't have wanted his son to sit upon the family throne without earning it.

Elizabeth came bounding into the hall and launched herself into Charles' arms. Despite the poison still oozing out of his pores, her presence brightened his heart. It always did. There was something both pure, but also deeply sad, about Elizabeth, and when he played with her, she always beamed bright. Sometimes it felt like the only thing he was capable of succeeding at on his own, though he rarely let his shortcomings get in the way of enjoying life.

As he grinned and greeted his baby sister, Irish Colleen snorted in disgust.

"I missed you," Elizabeth said as she dangled from his arms. At eleven, she was too big now to be held like she used to love. He swung her up over his back, fighting the wave of sickness that came over him at the quick movement.

"I always miss you, Sweet Lizzy," he said back and bounced her higher on his shoulders. What did the opinion of a stranger at Tulane matter when he was a hero in the eyes of someone so sweet, so pure?

As his sister curled over his back, Charles locked eyes with his mother. The brief smile that returned to her face when Elizabeth came in had melted back into simmering rage.

This isn't over, her eyes said. She turned and went back into the kitchen, where the smell of roast cooking nearly sent his stomach over the edge.

"You really messed up this time, Huck," his sister Colleen said from behind him. Where had she even come from? She always had a way of appearing from the shadows to pass judgment. It was like she'd forgotten they should be on the same side.

Charles ignored her and turned himself into an airplane, flying his baby sister around the house, fueled by her innocent squeals of joy.

CHAPTER 3

Daydream Believer

Maureen Deschanel was losing her mind, and it was her mother's fault.

She was fairly certain the process began somewhere around kindergarten and swooped in with hurricane force when her father succumbed to cancer. His death was an avoidable one, and another notch on the list of reasons Maureen loathed her mother. That Irish Colleen had helped August Deschanel keep his illness a secret until his death meant she had all but signed his death warrant. In a family of healers, death from disease in middle-age was a foolish end and an avoidable one. And further proof, in Maureen's mind, that her mother not only didn't understand the family she married into, but also secretly—or not so secretly—loathed them.

Irish Colleen had the means to save her husband and instead she watched him die a terrible death.

She insisted to her seven children she was honoring her husband's wishes. Only Maureen knew why her father opted out of magical intervention. Only Maureen knew because only Maureen could still see August Deschanel, and only Maureen could still talk to him. Only Maureen could still see and talk to August Deschanel because only Maureen was spiraling further and further away from her sanity.

August having his reasons for wanting to die a natural death did not exonerate Irish Colleen from allowing it to happen, though.

A knock sounded on her bedroom door.

"I'm studying!" she shrieked, rustling open her algebra textbook. The hard, cold cover slapped against her bare thigh.

"Dinner in ten!" called back Evangeline. Her heavy combat boots clopped along the cypress boards as she moved down the line of bedrooms with way too much enthusiasm. Maureen could almost picture her wild hair and obnoxious sense of purpose as she did her mother's bidding.

"I'd just as soon choke on my own vomit than eat that woman's food," Maureen muttered. She flipped through the pages with such force she ripped small tears. Good. Let them send her mother the bill. She ripped several more before slicing her finger.

"Hell's bells!" She sucked on her finger and continued on more carefully.

"You shouldn't speak of your mother that way," Maureen's father said.

Maureen leaped back in shock and slammed her head against the oak headboard. "Daddy, *God bless America*, what have we talked about? You can't just appear out of nowhere like... like a ghost. You'll give me a heart attack."

"I'm always here, Maureen, even when you can't see me."

"And yet, I'm the only one who *can* see you," she mused, thumbing angrily, but more carefully, through every chapter when she knew the one she wanted was near the back. She checked her wounded finger, saw it was still bleeding, and stuck it back in her mouth. "Because I'm a freak of nature. We all are."

"You're wrong. You're a Deschanel, and there's no greater blessing."

"Is that why you chose to die?" Tears rolled down her face as the anger blossomed through her fingertips. This topic of conversation always went nowhere fast, because dead August had collected enlightenment and wisdom along the way. He refused to let her wallow, when it was entirely her right. She could never decide whether she was ultimately comforted by his presence or enraged by the limitations of it. His arrivals tore her emotions down the seams and sewed them back together in haphazard, mismatched fashion, leaving her without her bearings and even more broken every time.

"You know why I chose to die."

"All I know is you chose to leave us."

"I chose to accept the fate God intended for me."

"I don't believe in God. I watch the news."

"My Sweet Maureen. Everything is linear in your eyes. The world is not so black and white."

Maureen didn't turn to face him. Seeing her dead father was her only tether to her sanity, and it was also the wind nudging her further off the edge.

"Be nice to your mother at dinner, Sweet Maureen. She hurts in ways you can't understand."

The tears ran down Maureen's cheeks unabated. She spun on her father, and the solidity, the realness of him, trapped her breath in her chest. "Yeah? She's not the only one."

Her father smiled sadly and then faded into the soft air of her bedroom.

"Five minutes!" Evangeline screamed. Thud, thud, thud went the soldier.

"Up yours," Maureen said. Evangeline enjoyed lording her two extra years in this world over Maureen, and Maureen wasn't about to let her take her licks that easily. Down the hall, a new horror appeared, escalating in obscene volume as Elizabeth turned on her Partridge Family record that made Maureen want to throw herself down the stairs *every single time.* There was no use yelling at her anymore. Elizabeth was such an odd kid that she hadn't the faintest idea why no one else wanted to hear her ridiculous music. At least her Herman's Hermits phase was over.

MAUREEN TURNED UP THE VOLUME ON HER OWN RECORD player and Carly Simon drowned out the world beyond her bedroom.

Her hand came to a rest at page 378. Maureen had no inkling what the text on the page meant. She was failing algebra and had no interest in improving. Maureen knew she would never have a use for it, because beautiful housewives had no use for math or other trivial subjects better suited for the man caring for her.

She smiled and sighed as she ran her fingers over the rough lines in the delicate petals of the dried rose stuck near the spine.

"Peter," she whispered. He was a secret not even her father knew, not that he could do much about it in his current state. If any of her family still among the living found out... well, she couldn't even let herself think of it. She had never known trouble like the reveal of Peter Evers would bring.

I'll take you away from here, Sweet Maureen. Peter's words, whispered in the steamed backseat of his tiny sports car. His sweaty, taught body pressed over the top of her, every jerky movement taking her away from the fourteen-year-old living with a deep, dark secret, yearning for escape. Wishing with every tendril of her soul that she was someone else, somewhere else.

She thought it odd that the only two men in her life who loved her both called her Sweet Maureen, but she believed it was a sign that they were the only ones she could trust. It made sense, in a way few things in her life ever did.

Maureen loved the hardness of his pectorals in her soft palms. They conveyed strength. Safety. *Don't say it if you don't mean it, Mr. Evers.*

Call me Peter. You're done with the eighth grade, Sweet Maureen. I'm not your teacher anymore.

MADELINE HAD ALREADY GONE FULL EMPATH BY THE TIME Maureen made it into the dining room. She braced herself for the incoming theatrics.

"Four dead, Mother! I felt each one, deep in the marrow of my bones!"

Maureen rolled her eyes so hard her sockets ached and grabbed a plate. "Here we go," she hissed under her breath.

"Maureen," Irish Colleen warned. "Maddy..." Long sigh. The one all the Deschanel children knew all too well, for it came at the moments where their mother was about to disappoint them in some profound way. "It's a terrible thing, what happened at Kent State. Truly horrible. But the damage is done. What will going to Ohio do except put you behind in school even more?"

"School?" The question came out somewhere between a scream and a sob. "This happened *at* a school, Mother. Don't you understand?"

Another sigh. Irish Colleen handed Elizabeth and Colleen plates. "I'm afraid I don't, Madeline. And this isn't a suitable dinner subject."

"Not a..." Spittle flew from Madeline as she whipped her head around in disgust. Maureen almost felt bad for her. If there was any of the seven who felt the pain of living under this roof as much as Maureen, it was Madeline. But Madeline was an insufferable cow who had no emotional self-control, and this erased any empathy Maureen managed to muster.

It was too bad, because it would have been nice to have an ally... even one sibling she got along with, and could confide in on a sleepless night.

"Sit," Irish Colleen demanded. They all did, even agitated Madeline. Augustus slid in quietly just as the hands linked for evening prayer. He flashed a guilty look to Irish Colleen for being late, but her focus was elsewhere.

"Where's Charles?" Irish Colleen asked. She shook her head before anyone could answer. The answer was the same most nights. "Augustus, will you lead us?"

"Let up, will you?" Maureen hissed at Madeline, who crushed her hand in hers.

Augustus hung his head. "Bless us, oh Lord, and Thy gifts,

which we are about to receive, through Thy bounty. Through Christ our Lord we pray. Amen."

"Amen," everyone but Madeline repeated.

"Pass the bread please, Maddy," Irish Colleen said. Tension choked the air.

"No."

"What did you say? No, we're not doing this tonight. Only one of us is the parent, Madeline, and you should count your blessings it's not you." She closed her eyes. Shook her head with a look toward the ceiling. "I can't remember the last time I actually slept."

"Here you go, Mama," Elizabeth said sweetly and handed the basket across her sisters.

"Don't think I've forgotten about your day, missy."

"Can't stay out of trouble, eh Lizzy?" Maureen taunted, tearing her roll in half. She would never miss an opportunity to keep her mother's ire pointed at someone other than herself.

"It's none of your business," Elizabeth returned. She stabbed her peas hard enough to scratch the plate with her fork. The screech that followed was horrible. Augustus winced.

"We'll discuss it tonight." Irish Colleen put an end to the conversation.

"Let's talk about something happy," Colleen suggested. Maureen had a fresh new eye roll for her oldest sister, who was always all too eager to be on the side of authority. Maureen suspected she didn't even know what it was like to be a kid. "Like Evangeline's teacher suggesting she skip a grade. What an amazing honor!"

"That's not happy news," Evangeline said. "I'll be a freak."

"Too late," Maureen said.

"You won't be a freak," Colleen soothed. *So reasonable. So perfect. I hate you.* "You'll graduate sooner, be in college sooner. Who wouldn't love that?"

Everyone, even Irish Colleen, looked at her like she was completely mad.

"If you think it's so great, why didn't you skip a grade?" Evangeline returned.

"She wasn't *asked,*" Maureen quipped. "Sucking up to your teachers doesn't automatically make you a genius."

"Maureen, remember yourself!" Irish Colleen flared. "What's gotten into you tonight?"

"You ask her that every night," Madeline said as she stared at the food on her plate, untouched. "As if you expect everything to change when nothing does. Nothing ever changes."

"Just like how you whine about some new crisis every night as if you're the goddamned Lord and Savior of the world," Maureen whipped back. She pulled her shoulders erect. "Your head might just fall off your shoulders if you tried to have a normal evening."

"She's an empath," Augustus said evenly. He set his fork on the plate. "You don't have to agree with what she's saying, or going through, to accept it."

"Shocking! You always take her side!"

"I'm only trying to help you understand."

"Help me understand? Or using your powers of persuasion on me?"

"I've never done that," Augustus defended. He looked wounded. "I wouldn't."

"So you say. How would I know?"

"Back to Evangeline," Colleen chimed in.

"Fuck Evangeline." Maureen threw her napkin on her plate. "And fuck you, Augustus, and you, Colleen, and yeah, even you, Lizzy. And *especially* whiny Madeline."

"Mau*reen*!" Irish Colleen yelled after her, but Maureen was gone, mentally, emotionally, completely. Now that she'd tasted a life outside of her own, her tolerance for her family had shorter frays and quicker explosions.

She ran down Sixth until she hit St. Charles Avenue, as fast as her legs could take her. Rain blinded her and ripped through her clothes, but it only quickened her stride and her resolution. She didn't stop until she reached the dime store at the corner of Jackson.

She fumbled in her jeans for some change and dropped it into the payphone.

Twenty minutes later, she hopped in Peter's car and they sped off in the direction of her future.

MAUREEN THOUGHT SHE WAS SO CLEVER. SO WORLDLY, so wise, with her way-too-old-for-her boyfriend, a secret she wore with smug, haughty self-indulgence, suggesting she was far too cunning for anyone to ever discover what she was doing when no one was paying attention.

Madeline had always been able to sense shifts in her siblings. She couldn't read minds, perhaps, but she could read emotions, and when you possess such an affliction you get used to studying the people around you, learning how to differentiate their periods of normalcy from the peaks and valleys of trauma and joy. Some were easier to detect changes in than others. Augustus had presumably one prevailing emotion at all times, and that was a steady, even focus. Occasionally he dipped into worry, especially where Madeline was concerned, but he very rarely blipped too high or low on the radar. When he did, you knew something was invariably wrong, and there was good cause to pay attention.

Others, like Maureen, like Evangeline, or sweet Lizzy, ran the gamut on a near-daily basis. Wild swings that could make a person dizzy to follow them.

Madeline wasn't judging, exactly. Not about this. She may find other reasons to disconnect her empathy from her siblings, but as she herself was all over the place most of the time, she could relate to them on this, if nothing else.

Even those with a dramatic range still had cues that grabbed Madeline's attention. In Maureen's case, she existed in a perpetual state of angst, to varying degrees, but rarely held onto any joy for more than a fleeting moment.

When Maureen's elation lasted not only hours, but days, and then weeks, Madeline knew something had happened. Shifted. She listened closer with her sixth sense and discovered that beyond joy, she found love. Or lust, more probably, because love had a soft evenness about it, as far as emotions went, where lust spiked all over the place, erratic and unpredictable.

From there, it took very little effort to uncover the cause. Madeline only needed to ask her classmates if they had heard of her freshman sister dating anyone. One of them—David if she recalled, though it wasn't important—took a double hit from the joint and held his answer with his smoke. He blew them out together. "Don't you know? She's fucking that middle school teacher... he teaches English, maybe? Shit, it's been a while. Quivers... Beavers..."

"*Evers*," answered another, probably Edie, reaching for what was left of the dwindling roach. "Don't bogart, man, come on."

Mr. Evers, who interestingly taught an elective class to eighth graders on the finer messages of Shakespeare, who was married, who had children, who was at least forty.

Could it really be that he was carrying on a relationship with Maureen? Forget that he was her teacher, forget that he was three times her age and married. What grown man would find himself enraptured with the childish grievances of a young girl who could potentially pass for eight if age was measured on an emotional spectrum? Why Maureen, of all the choices? Was it because she *was* so immature? That other girls her age weren't falling for whatever trap he laid?

Madeline knew she should report it. To her mother, at a minimum, but what she should really do is find a payphone and call it in to the authorities. Mr. Evers was at best a criminal, and at worst, a predator, and his behavior needed to stop, even if it ripped apart his family and life. Both would be his own fault. Life was a series of choices and results.

Instead, she couldn't muster within her the concern she knew she should possess for her sister's well-being. She had learned long ago that her capacity for concern for others had limitations in the way others didn't have, because to absorb the emotions of others put herself in high alert, and even danger. Maybe when the world stopped spending all its energy in killing each other she would have time and room in her heart for the trivial affair between her sister and her old teacher. It would be over before anyone was the wiser, anyway. No way that old coward was leaving his wife for a kid.

Madeline cleared her mind of her sister, who had only been there to begin with because of that knowing smile she flashed as she skipped by in the hallway, wearing her uniform a size too small. No, there were far more important things in life than correcting the course of a vapid, clueless child.

"Earth to Maddy," Edie said through a cough of smoke. "Did you hear me? You in?"

"Saturday morning. Ten. Be there or be square," David added with his lazy pothead grin that she wished he would stop employing. She hung with him because he had access to the best drugs and the best information, but it burned her heart because she knew he was an activist only because he believed it to be socially "in." His actual passions changed with the wind... or the smoke, as it were.

"I need to ask my mother," Madeline said, without much hope. She didn't know why she continued to ask. The answer was always no. It would never be yes until the day she stopped asking, and start taking action.

Like a true warrior of justice.

IRISH COLLEEN WASN'T HOME.

"Jesus, where the hell is she?" Madeline asked Evangeline, who sat spread-legged on a chair in the dining room, face pressed into a textbook.

Evangeline shrugged without looking up.

"She didn't say?"

"I didn't ask."

"Well, why not?"

Evangeline closed her eyes. Her neck sank into her shoulders as she affected a heavy sigh of exasperation. "Because not everything is a national emergency for me like it is for you," she huffed. With a dramatic smack, she slammed closed her calculus book and marched up the stairs.

Madeline rolled her eyes. And they called her dramatic.

"She won't be home until late," Colleen said from behind her. Madeline nearly jumped. "I'm handling dinner tonight."

"Not tuna casserole, right?" That disgusting dish was the only thing her older sister apparently knew how to make.

Colleen flashed a guilty look. "It's just for one night."

Madeline brushed past her, intent on locking herself away until she could confront her mother. This wasn't the end of the world. She needed time to think, anyway, to conjure a better strategy, one that might actually get through to her stubborn mother this time. She needed to be on that bus Saturday, come hell or high water.

Colleen's brows knitted together. She reached out for Madeline's arm and pulled her back, lining them up face-to-face. "Everything okay? Maybe I can help in Mom's absence?"

Madeline snorted. "You can't help with this."

Her older sister wedged herself in the doorway. "I know what you think of me. That I take everything too seriously and don't know how to have fun."

Madeline twerked her mouth in response. "Can I go upstairs now?"

Colleen folded her hands into a tent over her mouth. "I'm more like Dad than Mom, you know. I get what you're trying to do, and I don't think you're foolish, like Mom does. I know you're compassionate. I know being an empath makes your already large heart hurt even more when you see and feel terrible things happening to others. If I can help, Maddy, I will."

She sensed that her sister's offer was authentic, but Madeline knew better than to blindly trust any of her siblings, except Augustus. Yet, what if Colleen *could* help her? Irish Colleen valued the opinion of her eldest daughter, enough that her words might be the difference between persuading Irish Colleen and alienating her once again.

So Madeline took a chance.

She told Colleen about the bus leaving Saturday for Washington, about the rally for Kent State. How they would also stand against Nixon, and the war, and all the other great injustices plaguing the country. They were too numerous to count, and every single one was etched upon her soul, because of who she was.

"Madeline..." Colleen's softness had dissolved. In its place was the rigid form of her mother, preparing to unleash some great tyranny upon her.

She was a fool. She'd taken a chance, and this had backfired spectacularly.

"You know what, Colleen? It's fine. I didn't need your permission anyway." Madeline pressed forward. She grunted when Colleen held her ground. "Let me through."

"Listen, I'm on your side, but you *have* to finish school," Colleen was saying, but Madeline was done hearing everyone around her continue to throw up barriers. While she was in school, people were dying. Wars were being fought. What was school in the face of all this?

"I can do both."

"It's a distraction."

"I don't want to hear it from you," Madeline snapped. "I get it from Mom all the damn time."

Colleen shook her head. "You don't understand. I'm on your side."

"The hell you are!"

"If you would just listen..."

"Listen? To more people telling me how *not* to be myself?"

Colleen's hand pressed into her bicep with what Madeline guessed was supposed to be some kind of comfort. Instead it burned. She shook her away.

"I want you to be yourself. But you need that diploma first. The world is different for women now, and we can't waste the chances given to us. Wouldn't you feel better out there saving the world if you knew you had a life to return to when you're done?"

"You say that as if you think activism is a hobby, not a way of life," Madeline spat. She backed away from her sister, into the counter. "It *is* my life."

"A way of life is still a choice," Colleen went on, forcing a reasonableness to her tone that only incensed Madeline further. "Sometimes in order to do the things we want, we must first do the things we need."

"None of you understand. I'm not clamoring to get to protests so I can feel good about myself, or to have something to talk about to the sewing circle. I'm not checking a box, Colleen. I *want to be in the world helping people for the rest of my life, because I must, because if I don't, I'll go insane!*"

Colleen's hand stretched out and slapped her. No sooner than she had, her face filled with dark regret. "I didn't mean to do that."

Madeline clutched her stinging face. Tears poured into the hot skin. "You know what would be nice? To have an older sister I could talk to. Who at least *tried* to understand me, and maybe even comfort me from time to time."

"I'm not trying to hurt you... I didn't mean..." Colleen's own face flushed red and she looked confused, and Madeline could see, and feel, that her sister did regret the action, but it didn't matter now. None of it mattered.

"What is it about me you hate so much? Are you afraid of me, because I'm so in tune with my emotions while you're afraid of yours? Is that it?" Madeline looked around for her schoolbag, which she'd dropped on the way in. She didn't care about the textbooks, but she needed her diary. "You've always been more of a sister to Evangeline, hell, even Lizzy. You've never stood by my side."

"If standing by your side means watching you throw your life away, I will never," Colleen said, seemingly recovered from her brief violence. "Look around you, Maddy! Our whole family is in the middle of a crisis. Elizabeth can't stop predicting the deaths of her poor classmates and their families. Charles is a ticking time bomb, and it's a matter of *when*, not if, he will go off. Augustus just hides his head in the sand like he's not even a part of this family, like none of it matters, and you're trying to run off to dangerous protests when you haven't even finished school! You can be mad at me, but I'm only trying to keep this family together."

Madeline laughed through her tears. "That's Mom's job... you know that, right?"

Colleen squared herself. "As long as Charles, Maureen, and you make it hard for Mama, then I'll do what I can to help her. She's doing this all alone, Maddy. She has no one."

"Alone? That makes two of us," Madeline cried and shoved her sister out of the way, bookbag in hand, bolting up the stairs. She smashed into Elizabeth on the way, who gave her a look so curious that Madeline stopped altogether.

"What is it?" she snapped, the venom in her voice leftover from her fight with Colleen.

Elizabeth started to say something, then dropped her eyes and returned to her room.

CHAPTER 4

A Night to Remember

Colleen wiped away the dark smears and paused before commencing her fourth attempt at eye makeup. She didn't know how to apply it properly on an average day, but her tears threw up a barrier greater than her lack of skill.

Agreeing to Rory's prom invitation was foolish and short-sighted. She was in no mood to put on a smiling face and surrender to whatever teenage antics awaited at the Roosevelt Hotel.

She folded into a heap on her vanity seat and buried her tear-stained face in her hands. This was hopeless. How could she even attempt joy, after how deep her rift with Madeline had grown? She never meant it to get that far. After the sting of her hand connecting with her sister's face, Colleen had never in her life wished more that she could rewind time by even a second.

And now even Maureen had joined in with the silent treatment. Maureen, who had never gotten along with Madeline, found alliance with her sister on their shared belief Colleen was a terrible sister. Augustus would always side with Madeline; she was his single weakness, unless you marked him down for being too serious. But Colleen was the same, so she did not.

Charles had always loathed her, and even he now took a stance on the matter of Colleen vs. Madeline, when he had never cared before. She suspected he was latching on to the opportunity to draw attention away from himself and capitalizing on a feud that had taken over the entire household.

None of them understood. Children were inherently selfish, even if not in any malicious way, and only Colleen could apparently see how their mother struggled to corral seven headstrong individuals and turn them into responsible adults with promising futures. Charles dismissed all of this, because he saw his position as Deschanel heir as a get-out-of-anything-free card. Colleen's sisters had also never known true consequence, for first August, and then, with hesitation, Irish Colleen, had sheltered them from what the world might bring to their door should they misstep too far. Irish Colleen was perpetually torn between protecting her children from anything too terrible and trying to teach them that those too terrible things could easily happen without the right measure of caution and prevention.

Colleen felt a kinship toward her long-suffering mother, and she didn't know if she was born with such maturity and seriousness, or if she had slowly grown into it because of her work on the Deschanel Magi Collective Council. She believed it would eventually pay off, that her life would be solid and safe because she chose to follow the path of rightness. But if this was true, why was she always so unhappy? So alone?

Deep in her soul, Colleen knew, had always known, that it would be her and not her two older brothers who stepped forward to lead this family one day. Charles would settle into his comfortable life as heir, August would bury his head in business, and Colleen would be left carrying the weight of her family on her shoulders. And if she failed, or chose not to step up to this challenge? Who else would do it? Surely not flighty, unmoored Madeline, or tempestuous Maureen. Evangeline might rise to the occasion, but her chaotic mind would never focus the way it needed in order to lead and inspire. Evangeline might stand at Colleen's side and be her anchor, but she herself would never be anchored for long. And poor, sweet Elizabeth would be tormented the rest of her life with seeing the inevitable sadness in her future.

No, it must be Colleen. And only she understood, and had the foresight to know, her actions today would inform the future. While her siblings were wrapped up in their own life, Colleen prepared her own for one of service to them, and everyone else sharing their blood. Most days, she embraced this. But with most of her family having turned on her, the bitterness boiled over until it escaped as unstoppable tears.

Hands rolled over her shoulders. Colleen raised her head and Evangeline smiled behind her in her reflection.

"Crying doesn't pair well with that red dress," Evangeline teased. She re-arranged pieces of Colleen's curls. "Can you calm down long enough for me to apply some eyeliner?"

Colleen laughed and sniffled. "Don't you have homework?"

Evangeline's eyes rolled. "I'm being skipped ahead a grade because I'm so far behind."

"Right." Colleen pulled a tissue from a box on the vanity and dabbed at her eyes. "I'm thinking maybe I won't go now."

Evangeline's shocked expression gaped back at her. "I can give you a dozen reasons, all based on logic, on why you should attend this developmental rite of passage, but even I can't pretend to care about the logic around sweaty, horny teenagers dancing and fawning over each other for several hours to nonsensical decorative choices, so here's something else. Rory is your friend, and he's going to be here any minute, with some shitty flower to pin on your boob, and a crazy wide smile because he got his crush to say yes to his proposition of sweaty, horny dancing."

"Why pursue a career in science with that command of language?"

Evangeline shrugged, missing the sarcasm. This was the thing about her genius sister. Her brilliant mind had no room for nuance. "It's only a few hours, Leena. Rory will be happy as a clam, you'll feel good about yourself, and there are strong odds you'll even be glad you went for your own reasons. But in either case, it's too late to back out now, so let's embrace one more social convention and get your makeup straight."

"It's hard to want to have fun, Evie, when your whole world is off-kilter."

"That's dramatic, Leena, and not your style," Evangeline pointed out, with a wry grin. "I know who you are. One day, they will, too. I could wax on about the psychological principles on the evolving nature of parent-child relationships, but you have a prom to attend."

Colleen wiped away the last of her tears. The redness in her eyes would fade, hopefully before Rory arrived, as Evangeline had said, with his crazy wide smile. "I don't like how this feels, Evie. But I can't change who I am. I can't stop wanting the best for everyone I love."

Evangeline ran a lighter over the charcoal pen. She lifted it to eye level, squinted, and then blew on the cooling tip. "Tonight isn't about them, Leena."

Colleen closed her eyes as the first of the warm coal swept over her lids. She steadied herself with measured breaths. In. Hold. Out. Slow. Her chest trembled as she released the sorrow.

"It's about you," Evangeline continued. She leaned back to examine her work. "This is *your* night. You can stress about those punks in the morning."

COLLEEN COULD NOT STOP ADJUSTING HER DRESS. SHE thought chiffon would be safe, but the designer had used too much and Colleen had the perpetual sensation her underwear was on display for all her classmates. Rory caught her shuffling and yanking and finally, amused, agreed to be her lookout for any sign of an impending wardrobe disaster.

This wasn't a tough assignment for him. He wouldn't, or couldn't, stop staring at her. Either as she sipped her punch from the plastic cup, or when he thought she was people watching.

Colleen had always been very aware of her surroundings and she didn't need to see Rory to feel his eyes on her.

The dynamic of her relationship with Rory Sullivan had evolved over the years. Their families were close. Charles' best friend was Rory's older brother, Colin. Their younger brother, Patrick, dated Madeline for a short time, and the youngest, Chelsea, was a sometimes friend of Maureen, when they weren't embroiled in some dramatic fight or another. August Deschanel once said he trusted the Sullivans more than his own blood. Their law firm was so deeply enmeshed in the Deschanel business that without that trust, they would be exposed in significant ways.

Colleen was more comfortable with Rory than many of her peers. It wasn't only that she'd grown up with him, or that he was a Sullivan. Like her, he took his studies seriously, for the most part, but he was one of the few people who didn't think Colleen's solemnity was foolish, or unimportant. He might tease her from time to time about having fun, but Rory understood her studies, her family, these were intrinsic, essential pieces of who she was. He often showed up with a snack from their favorite donut shop on St. Charles, and his school satchel, and they would spend their Saturday mornings studying for their respective classes in comfortable silence.

When Carolina was around, it was all about the fun and adventure, but when it was only Colleen and Rory, there was a quiet understanding that passed between them, where she felt both safe and understood.

But she did not at all know how to feel about the way he looked at her tonight.

Rory took the plastic glass she'd been coddling in her hands like a security blanket, and pulled her by the hand to the dance floor. Some Beatles song played, which she knew she should recognize but didn't. Madeline would. Hell, all her siblings would, even Augustus. Colleen was an utter failure as a teenager.

He had one of her hands folded in his, and the other at the small of her back. She was startled at the surge of intimacy this produced.

It was only her back, after all. Colleen shivered and pressed her face closer in, so he could not see her scandalized expression.

The musky, cloying scent of English Leather consumed her. She recognized it as the cologne Charles doused on his clothes before a date, and she supposed women must go wild for it, but the very mature cloud hanging over the moment left her confused. Had he worn it for her? She couldn't recall any specific scents reminding her of Rory, except the occasional hint of his deodorant, or the sweat clinging to his uniform after a lacrosse game.

"You look really beautiful tonight, Colleen," Rory said. His breath caught after the words were out. She felt his pulse through his hand.

"I feel silly," she replied and then chided herself. She was terrible with compliments, and this wasn't the time for that. "But thank you."

"Yeah, of course, this whole thing is silly," Rory said quickly. He followed his rushed words with a clipped laugh. "Lame central."

Colleen's own pulse was beyond her control. She wanted to tell him he looked handsome. And oh, he did. All Sullivan men were traditionally beautiful, with their dark hair and Irish green eyes bearing that look of loyal determination. But Rory possessed a softness that belied a special kindness. If he were a Deschanel, she would have thought he was an empath, for how connected he was to how others were feeling. All this he radiated to his exterior self, like an aura. Whoever married Rory Sullivan would be a fortunate woman. Probably Carolina, who undoubtedly would've been his date tonight if she were a senior.

"If…" Colleen swallowed her better sense, which told her any unguarded words would lead to regret. "If I was going to do anything lame with someone, I'm glad it's you."

Rory pressed his cheek to hers. She felt his smile as his soft skin stretched.

When the song ended, she tried to return to the seats behind the punch table, but Rory laced his hand in hers and led her farther into the floor. The slow song had changed to a fast one, something rock and roll, and Rory began to gyrate into some sort of dancing. Colleen at first thought he was being playful, but then the rest of her classmates launched into similar moves, and she realized *she* was the ridiculous one. The outsider. The one who didn't know how to be cool, or interesting.

Rory sensed her hesitation and pulled her into his arms, spinning her, dipping her. He took both her hands in his and his eyes said to trust him, to follow his lead. Colleen nearly tripped over her two left feet. She was clumsy and untested in social situations. She'd make a fool of them both.

But then her feet were moving, really moving, and she matched his strange bobbing and weaving in time. The rush that passed through her as she realized she was actually doing this propelled her faster and into a rhythm of even more precision and frenzy.

Colleen, you fool, you're dancing. And you're not that shabby, either.

Rory reached inside his jacket pocket and produced a shimmering silver vial. Colleen's eyes widened. It was a flask.

He unscrewed the lid and, with a wary glance to check for chaperones, tilted the flask back and let the clear liquid flow into his mouth.

Rory started to replace the lid and then looked at her. "I already know the answer, but..."

In exhilarated response, caught in the thrill of who she was then, not who she wanted to be, or who she was in the real world, she ripped the silver container from his hand and tossed back a swig of vodka.

As Colleen wiped her mouth with the back of her hand, Rory leaned in and kissed her. Her first kiss. Her first anything, with any boy. She looped her arm around his neck and abandoned herself to the moment, to Rory, to the night, to whatever it might bring next.

Her fingers struggled with the button on his pants. Who invented such buttons? How had he ever gotten the pants on to begin with?

Rory's kisses at her neck were too much. She needed more, and the burning between her legs was new, so new she didn't know any other way to satisfy it except ripping his pants from his body.

One strap of her dress lay down the middle of her arm. The zipper in the back was half-down, probably Rory's doing, but why was it not all the way down... why was it still on, when she wanted him so *bad,* and he wanted her, and...

Colleen's head spun. She stopped fumbling with his button and sat back on the bed to right herself.

Rory leaned forward and asked if she was okay, and after she assured him she was, of course she was, she was Colleen Deschanel and she was *always* okay, he kissed the rest of her rambling words right out of her mouth. She looked down to see his pants at his ankles and was relieved someone else had dealt with the troubling situation of Rory Sullivan's stubborn button.

Colleen snaked her arms behind her, but her hand grasped at skin or dress, but not zipper. It was pulled too far down for her to find it, and she groaned in desperation. She closed her eyes as the room spun again, the chair and table appearing on the ceiling, and the bed a world away.

Rory's arms came around her. He buried his face in her neck and she felt a significant release as her dress no longer held her in. It fell around her waist and then the room moved again as Colleen fell on her back and Rory came over her. His tie hung down his bare chest.

"I've been so, so very good," Colleen cooed. She didn't know where the words came from, or the next that she whispered as she tugged him down by his tie. "Why have you let me be so, so good, Rory?"

"Because you are perfect in my eyes, Colleen," Rory said. A crisp moment of sobriety passed between them, as he looked so intensely into her eyes, and as she heard his words not as a drunken senior, but as a woman embroiled in a very serious moment.

Colleen wrapped her legs around his waist, and Rory's eyes rolled back in his head. He moaned and fell atop her, ravishing her neck, chin, chest with kisses. He ripped at her bra and a sharp chill hit her as her nipple rolled between his lips. She wished he would bite it, bite her, consume her.

Something hard pushed at her panties. She knew the word. Knew what it was, and if she was to have it, she couldn't be afraid to say it. Cock. She let the word travel around her mind. Cock. Rory's cock. It was real, and this was real, and everything now was real, real, real...

His fingers pulled her panties aside and then this very real thing was happening completely, fully. His cock parted her throbbing flesh between her legs and she spread wider to allow, no, invite... demand. Colleen had never wanted anything more than she wanted Rory Sullivan to be inside her, taking away all the responsibility, the pain, the heartache.

As he moved, at first jerky and nervous, and then with the smooth fluidity of a man confident, Colleen wondered why she had been so hard on herself. So unwilling to let these experiences in. The world hadn't stopped, she was still Colleen, she was still breathing, even if her pulse was off the charts and the ecstasy... the pure, unabated pleasure...

When Rory shuddered and slowed his pace, she rolled her head to the side, exhausted, euphoric. She very distantly heard him whisper he loved her.

It was still dark outside when Colleen woke. Rory slept soundly on his stomach, arms spread to the side.

Her head throbbed. Stars appeared behind her eyes when she tried to sit forward. This must be a hangover, she thought, but the dizziness made her question instead whether she was still drunk. The tile on the clock ticked over. It was 2:27 a.m.

Another soreness appeared, this one between her legs. She was naked except for her underwear. She saw a flash of red chiffon at the end of the bed, where her dress hung half-on, half-off.

Where were they? She remembered arriving in the hotel room, but not how they'd gotten there. She squinted at the card by the phone. *Bourbon Orleans.* That was over a mile from the Roosevelt. Had they taken a cab? She could slap herself. Her family were long-time patrons of the hotel; they even had a room named for them. Word would reach her family before she could make her way home.

Colleen carefully stepped out of the bed and reached for the tattered dress, which was as clear a reminder as any of what had happened here only hours before. The bright red sat in homage, judging, like a scarlet letter. She clutched it to her chest, where her heart didn't know whether to beat swiftly or not at all, and stumbled into the bathroom.

She closed and locked the door behind her. She could not let Rory see her like this, but she realized, also, as she hovered over the toilet to wipe away the evidence of the night before, as she cast her eyes from the mirror, that she couldn't see *herself* this way.

Colleen flushed the paper down the commode but couldn't manage to pull herself back up. Rory. The bed. The dress. The stark, quiet bathroom of the hotel. None of this was as it should be.

This is your night, Evangeline had said, though she quite surely didn't have any of this in mind when she stated the reassurances with such confidence.

She reached for her hair. Half the curls had fallen out, and the other half stood atop her head, a further reminder of her shame.

Colleen had to leave. She had to be home, where she was safely herself, and ensconced within the world she knew best.

She dug around in her hair for the bobby pins she knew were still there. Then, slipping them in her mouth for holding, Colleen wrapped her hair in a tight bun, as tight as she could pull it, and one by one slipped the pins into place.

Better.

Colleen cast a forlorn gaze at the dress. It all came back to the dress. She couldn't bear to put it back on, but nor could she catch a taxi naked. Then she remembered Rory's dress shirt. On her, it would cover enough to get her home. He still had his jacket and pants, and wouldn't be helpless.

She suppressed the tears she only just realized were rolling down her cheeks. They wouldn't serve her here, in this moment. Whatever she had done, it could be fixed. The world could be righted. Only Colleen had this power, and she knew precisely how to wield it.

Quietly, she tiptoed around to Rory's side of the bed and fumbled for his shirt. There was little chance of waking him, but any chance was more than she was prepared for. To hold together her thin vestige of control, she needed no further obstacles.

Colleen stood at the door and watched him. She held her dress in one arm, and her heels in the other. Rory. Had she really? Had she done this?

As he slept, she understood she did not regret what she had done with Rory. If there was ever a man to give her virginity to, it was the only one she trusted with her truest self.

What she regretted was that the night happened as a result of her lack of control.

And, no matter her desires, she could never allow her control to slip so easily away again.

CHAPTER 5

The Heir, the Spare, and the Affair

Charles' relationship with his five sisters had always been contemptuous, excepting the gentle comradery he had with sweet Elizabeth. This was largely their fault, as he saw things, and he very rarely saw things in ways that put him in the direct line of responsibility. Not that his reasons weren't perfectly sound, as far as he was concerned.

Colleen had a stick up her ass thicker and larger than the oak arms in Audubon Park.

Madeline's misguided attempts at philanthropy showed, in contrast to what she believed, just how little she knew of the world from her magnolia-sheltered mansion.

Evangeline's intelligence made him feel even stupider than he likely was, which was on good days an annoyance and on most days too keen a reminder that he, as the heir, was not the best and brightest at everything.

And Maureen—unlike Colleen, who was focused; unlike Madeline, who had a tender heart; unlike Evangeline, who was smart as hell—had so few redeeming qualities he wondered if she hadn't accidentally fallen into their family after being switched at birth at the hospital. Those sorts of things did happen. He'd seen it on the evening news.

But Charles loved his sisters, because there was no power stronger and more binding than blood. He was the heir of this blood, and that came with a certain set of responsibilities, even if most of his responsibilities had been shoved aside in the name of living as he saw fit. August had impressed at least that on his eldest son, if he'd impressed nothing else. *They are yours now, and may you never forget it.*

Charles didn't know the first thing about protecting others, despite that protection was clearly a key part of looking after one's family. There was, of course, a certain protection extending from their name alone. This was why he'd never *really* be kicked out of college, despite Irish Colleen's histrionic predictions. But their name would not protect his sisters from being assaulted, or from heartbreak. For Charles, the world fit most neatly into a set of absolutes, and when he strained to break down what it meant to be the heir, what his father truly intended with the words, *they are yours now,* it made the most sense to him to apply a literal interpretation.

He was their bodyguard.

Though he couldn't remember precisely when he'd set some of his friends to the task of following the girls, he thought it was probably around the time Colleen first started bursting out of her argyle sweaters. Charles had never met a friend who wouldn't bend over backward to please him—except Colin, but Colin was Colin, and maybe that's why Charles liked him best—so it was no effort at all to find a couple guys to keep an eye on his sisters for him, just every now and then, to make sure there wasn't anything Charles might need to get concerned with.

This was how Charles came to find out about Colleen spending the night in a hotel with Colin's little brother, Rory.

Rory hung around the house a lot. Charles knew it was a lot, because he himself was hardly home, and whenever he *was* home, so was Rory Sullivan, in his colorful sweaters knitted by his mother, with that goofy smile that never seemed to disappear. That Irish Colleen let the kid hang out in her eldest daughter's room with the door closed was either a testament to her trust in Colleen, or her acceptance that Colleen would just as soon cut a finger off than do anything fun or interesting. God forbid.

Charles didn't think Rory had fooled around with his sister in the Deschanel home, and this was more a credit to Colleen than the Sullivan kid, but he could think of only one reason you took a woman to a hotel room. They could do smart, nerdy stuff, like speak math to each other, anywhere, which is probably as far as things went sequestered in Colleen's pristine room.

No, Rory Sullivan had taken Charles' sister to a hotel room to fuck her, and that could not stand.

It would have been nothing at all for Charles to obtain the room number from the concierge, simply by flashing his name as leverage. Reminding them the Deschanels had a room in this hotel reserved especially for them at all times, that couldn't be rented to anyone else under any circumstance. Yes, he was *that* Charles Deschanel, and no one wanted trouble. But his buddy had been thorough, following the drunken couple all the way to the ninth floor, and dutifully noting what room they disappeared through. He could have left out the details about Colleen's dress hanging off her as she urged Rory to be quicker about it, before stealing the key and unlocking the room herself.

He didn't suppose knocking would have the same effect as bursting in like a commando, so what Charles did need was a key, and a breach of security was a tougher hurdle than a slip of information.

The young kid at the front desk was an old classmate, which he immediately noted as exceptionally fortunate. He recognized the black glasses and ten thousand freckles painting his face like a disastrous explosion at the brown paint factory. This International Club reject was all too happy to find himself a silent conspirator of Charles Deschanel. Probably daydreaming about what a friendship with such a person could bring; the adventures they would go on.

"You remember me?" The kid actually said it, oblivious to how pathetic and ridiculous even hoping for such a thing made him seem.

"Of course, man. Of course." He read the nametag. "My man, Jimmy."

Charles didn't disavow the kid of these fantasies, nor did he have any shame in using an unsaid promise to get what he wanted. A person had to employ what tools they had at their disposal, and those with too much compunction to do so never made it very far in the world. That had *not* been a lesson of August Deschanel, but a man could learn from more than just his father.

Key in hand, Charles retraced the steps of his goody-goody sister and her horny boyfriend. The growing lump in his belly was one of a vague nauseated disgust, like he'd eaten eggs before nine in the morning, and it only expanded when he realized he would have to do this very same thing for four other sisters, at some point, or many points. A job that would never end.

He hesitated just outside the hotel room door with a puzzled grimace. Hesitation was not a very familiar reaction for Charles, who was often—sometimes rightly, sometimes unfairly—accused of putting his temper before his temperance. But it wasn't his anger that stilled him. Rather, a whisper of good sense pointed out to him that he might come upon his sister in a compromising position and inherit an image embedded in his mind that couldn't be expelled with all the coke in the world.

"To hell with it," he muttered and turned the key. If Colleen was in a bad way, that was between her and the Lord, and she was fortunate her brother cared enough to save her from herself.

Charles flung the door wide. It bounced off the rubber doorstop and nearly smacked him right in the face, but he deftly stepped through and left it swinging. He didn't immediately see Colleen, which was almost a relief, but Rory lay spread across the bed, naked as the day he was born, sheets twisted around his ankles. The brazen audacity of the kid fired up Charles' rage and jumped it into the next level. Naked. Naked because he had knowingly and calculatedly taken Charles' sister to this room only hours before, with the full intent to screw her brains out. Naked, without a care or concern, without consequence.

Charles stormed across the room like an angry bull.

He ripped the remainder of the bedding off the mattress and dragged the Sullivan kid by his limp arm. Rory's eyes flew open, followed by his stupid mouth, followed by what Charles could see was him working his mind around some kind of answer to this abrupt shift in reality.

"You fucking dare touch my sister, you hooligan," Charles seethed, and Rory bounced half off the bed and onto the thin carpet on the floor. He searched around for something to cover himself, but Charles shoved him away, and he half-skittered, half-flew on to his back. His hands scrambled for purchase, and he crawled around backward like a drunken crab, until he hit the paisley green armchair in the corner.

"Jesus, Charles!" Rory, in the absence of any other defense, threw his hands up over his face to shield himself. He drew his knees high to protect other assets.

"Where is she?" Charles ripped one pillow off the bed, then another, and chucked them at Rory, drawing from his days as a pitcher for Brother Martin's varsity baseball team. The plush pillows lost momentum in mid-air, but this only pissed him off more, and he chucked the next one so hard something in his arm started to burn. "Where is my sister?"

"She left," Rory replied as he dodged the assault. Even after Charles had run out of pillows, his arms didn't ease. "Early. I don't know. She didn't say anything, and I thought maybe she wanted it that way, so I didn't stop her."

"Wham, bam, thank you, ma'am?" Charles lobbed at the cowering Rory. He searched for something else to throw, but the remaining items in the room were of a much heavier nature. The television. The clock. A good direct hit with those would probably land him in jail, and he needed at least another week or two of distance between the call from Tulane and yet another questionable incident with his name on it.

"No! No, it wasn't like that at all." Rory plied one arm away and squinted as he looked up at Charles. "Colleen is my *friend*. I would never hurt her."

"Just fuck her and dump her."

"We aren't going steady, or anything like that, it just happened."

Charles eyes stretched open so wide he wondered if it was scientifically possible for them to pop out of his sockets. And if they did fall out, could he shove them back in? Would they still work, or would he need to find a doctor to perform some rare procedure to grant him his eyesight back? Evangeline would know. "That's what a dick says when he's messed with a girl."

Rory winced again, but Charles had nothing left to throw. "I wouldn't mess with Colleen. And I pity the idiot who ever tries. You and I both know she never does anything she doesn't want to do. I didn't pressure her. She came here because she wanted to."

Spittle flew from Charles' mouth as he prepared to launch some other unpleasant counterattack, but Rory's logic had him stuck. "So why did she leave?"

"I told you, I don't know. You know her, she's afraid of letting go and having fun, and maybe she felt bad about that. I heard her leave, passed back out, and only just woke up again when you burst in here like Steve McQueen. I plan to go see her this afternoon and find out what's going on with her. Reassure her it wasn't just a... fun night for me."

"Fun," Charles repeated, but he gave serious consideration to Rory's words. Colleen was even more stubborn than he was, in many ways, if not different ways. "Does Colin know what you're into with my sister?"

Rory shrugged. He pulled himself into a more erect seated position, but at an angle, where he could easily shift back into a defensive stance. "He knows I like her."

"I came here to kill you."

"I figured as much." Long breath.

"No one fucks with my sisters."

"I figured that much as well." Rory chanced a reach forward

and pulled the sheet up and over him. "Look, if you're worried about your sisters, maybe check into what Maureen has gotten into."

"Maureen?" Charles wrinkled the center of his face together. This wasn't part of the plan. His immediate reaction to being caught unawares was fresh anger. "What the hell are you talking about?"

Rory shook his head. "I don't know if it's true. I've just heard things."

"Things? What things?" Charles' temples throbbed. He reached up to massage them, as if that ever helped.

"She's possibly in over her head with some guy." Rory looked as if he deeply regretted mentioning this and wanted to retreat under the chair and disappear entirely. "I don't know a lot about it, to be honest. But people talk, and her name has been coming up a lot."

"Why tell me now? Why not before?"

"Our father, he's always told us not to gossip. To never repeat something that isn't backed by evidence. I don't have any evidence, man, I've only heard rumors. Might be nothing."

"Nothing," Charles repeated, but suddenly had a very acute feeling it was not nothing at all.

CHARLES HAD NO PLAN WHEN HE LEFT THE HOTEL, ONLY a fresh, roiling, and mostly confused wrath that he had very little understanding of, or control over. He'd rushed to the hotel with one form of vengeance in mind, one that was very clear in his head, and was now on his way home with a very unclear plan, with even more unclear details.

He'd hoped to be at the Playboy Club by midday for some of his favorite antics, but that seemed less and less likely.

Maureen. The girl was trouble, no doubt. She had no focus in school, which Charles could not himself judge without some heavy hypocrisy, but she was also not very nice, or bright about the world in general. Maureen approached everything in her life with an open hostility that made Charles uncomfortable, even when he himself was in a state. She was pretty, though. Maybe the prettiest of all the Deschanel girls, if she could bring herself to wipe the constipated look from her face from time to time. Charles used to joke that she'd make a good trophy wife, a dig at her apparent lack of any other useful skills, but now, when she was more woman than girl, that joke was not nearly as funny.

Fourteen. When he was fourteen, he'd started fucking his way through the Sacred Heart Academy, though he didn't garner the momentum he desired for another couple years, when the girls finally came around to the idea that what the nuns didn't know wouldn't hurt them.

Charles still saw Maureen as a child, even after she'd traded bobby socks and matching pleats for cropped tops and minis. He supposed this shift reminded him more of a child playing dress-up than one growing up, but if Rory's words were true, Maureen might be more like Charles, at fourteen, than he thought.

Rory could be bluffing, or lying. That was still a possibility. He'd certainly been eager to deflect Charles' anger somewhere other than himself. But he could have done that in other ways, or chose a more likely sister to be in trouble, like Madeline, because when wasn't that girl in trouble? Maureen's name was what gave Charles pause and led him to think there might be truth in the rumors.

He decided the best person to ask about this was Augustus.

Charles and Augustus could not be two more different people. Augustus did not need to point this out for Charles to be acutely and persistently aware of it. His perfect grades, fastidious manners, conservative dress, and unfailing dedication to anything he put his mind to. All these things served as signs directing the neon "perfect son" sign right over Augustus' head, while Charles clung to the important designation of being the heir, and the slightly better looking brother—Rory *had* just likened him to Steve McQueen, after all, when he could have as easily said Charles Bronson. Augustus could cure cancer and rid the world of hunger, but Charles was still the Deschanel heir, and that was that.

Or so he told himself.

When he found himself in need of aid, or advice, he invariably found himself in the confidences of his younger brother. Being around Augustus made him feel smarter himself, and perhaps more grounded, especially when he knew these things would never change his position in the household as the first. Smart, grounded friends made a man these things, too. This was why his friendship with Colin had flourished, while his friendships with the boys more like him had fizzled.

Augustus was studying in the dining room when Charles arrived, whirling through the house like a fresh spring storm. Augustus set down his pencil and pulled his glasses to the top of his head.

“I always know when it’s you.”

Charles smirked. “Yeah? Why?”

“I find myself searching my brain to make sure I know the most efficient hurricane evacuation routes out of the city.”

“Very funny. Can you see me laughing?”

“I can see you’re feeling something intense,” Augustus said, with just a hint of bemusement.

Charles dropped his arms on the oak table and leaned in. “Where’s Mom?”

“Making groceries. She took Lizzy about an hour ago.”

“And the other girls?”

“Out, except Colleen, who’s sleeping off what I imagine is a killer hangover.”

“Well,” Charles said, drawing the word out as he dropped into the seat, “I just returned from the Bourbon Orleans, where Rory Sullivan and Colleen shared a room for the night.”

Augustus’ brows shot up. “Well! That explains the look she gave me when she came in.”

“What time was that?”

“Just past three?”

Charles slapped his hands on the table. “Our sister came in at three in the morning and you didn’t ask her why?”

"It was prom night," Augustus said with a shrug. "And she's Colleen. I might have stopped Maddy, or Maureen."

"Maureen," Charles said. "Fucking Maureen. I don't even know why I'm bothering to ask you, since you didn't seem to notice or care that Colleen came in doing the walk of shame at three in the goddamn morning, but have you heard anything about what our dear Maureen has been up to?"

Augustus scrunched his face. "She's failing a couple of her classes. Not long ago, she just ran away, right in the middle of dinner. But she's at that age, I guess. Hormones, maybe?"

Charles' head shook in a furor. "*No,* brother, we're on the subject of late night sex calls, so why would I be talking about grades and dinner?"

His brother laughed. "What the devil does Maureen have to do with the subject of late night sex calls?"

"You tell me."

"Charles, I'm really busy, so unless you have something specific, or—"

"She's into something bad. I know it. Rory told me so."

"Rory?" Augustus curled the corner of his mouth into a quick smile. "Before or after he had sex with our sister and you threatened his life?"

"I didn't threaten his life."

Augustus' look conveyed his skepticism quite well.

"Even if I did, something feels fishy about this. Mom has been so busy trying to keep Madeline from joining the Peace Corps, and Lizzy can't stop predicting the deaths of her friends' daddies. Evangeline is too smart for her own good. I just don't think it's impossible that when we were busy with other things, Maureen decided to have her own little fun."

"She's fourteen," Augustus said with the dry arrogance of someone who was boring as hell at the age of fourteen.

"And she's more like me at fourteen than you at fourteen. Think about *that* for a moment."

Augustus appeared to be giving the entire encounter some

serious thought. He drew in several breaths, then released them in short intervals as he looked around the room, as if he expected some unseen ally to arrive and provide backup. "If she is up to something with a boy, it needs to stop. But if you confront her, throwing around accusations, we both know she won't tell you anything."

"So, you haven't heard anything."

"No! If I had, you don't think I would've put a stop to it by now?"

"I don't think you care about much, except studying. And Maddy."

Augustus crossed his arms. "You should care about studying, too. As for Maddy, I'm trying to keep her from dropping out of school and ruining her life. Yes, I care about that. You should, too. She's the one you need to be concerned about. Not Colleen having a little fun for a change, or Maureen throwing normal teenage tantrums."

"Maddy is dramatic. And you eat it right up." Charles mimed licking each of his fingers with great flourish.

"Are we done here?"

Charles pushed back the chair so far it rattled into the china cabinet. He stood, keeping his eyes on Augustus as he slowly backed out of the room.

"I'll get the answers. And when I do, you'll be eating your words, Spare."

"Spare?"

"I'm the heir, you're the spare." Charles had heard this from some girl he dated for a night. She'd rambled on about a documentary she'd watched on the British royal family, and this idea that they always tried for at least two sons, in case the first one fell ill, or died. The heir, and the spare. He liked this. He'd use it as much as he could.

"Whatever you say, Huck," Augustus said, less ruffled than Charles was hoping, and returned to his textbook.

. . .

MAUREEN LOST HERSELF TO THE FRENETIC RHYTHM OF what Peter liked to call, "lovemaking, baby. Not sex. Not with us." It was always fast, never slow, which confused Maureen, because in the movies she sometimes snuck from Charles' room, the ones her mother would ground her forever for if she learned she'd watched, it was always the other way around. Lovemaking was slow, measured, with a tenderness that reminded her a little of the way a healthy family might interact. Sex was fast, rough, and impersonal, suggesting to Maureen it didn't matter who was there, or why. A means to an end.

But Peter assured her these five-minute, feverish sessions in the back of his car, with his zipper undone but his pants intact, and her dress hiked up half around her neck, were how he showed his love. She wondered, if this was his love, how long did sex last? The length of a sneeze?

Maureen had her doubts, but did it really matter? If this was how he showed love, it was a step up, for sure. Her only experience with love before him was her mother's shrill demands that Maureen fit her perfect mold, and whatever *this* was, whatever Peter thought of her, she walked away feeling better than she did when she left home.

At thoughtful intervals, Maureen released her own contributions to the act, a series of grunts and moans, of begging for more, calling him daddy, which he insisted made the love even stronger. It was pretty weird, but she didn't care. All that mattered to her was that Peter had promised to leave his wife and marry her, and she wouldn't do anything that might cause him to change his mind. If that meant pretending to enjoy their lovemaking, or calling him strange nicknames, she would sign up a thousand times over.

For this was her only escape from the madness. The only place her own father wouldn't follow, and for as much as she missed him, this place of limbo, where he was here, but not really, never in the way he once was, was somehow worse than standing at the Deschanel Tomb in the middle of a summer New Orleans storm and saying her final goodbyes.

When she married Peter, she worried her father might then start showing himself again. She had all sorts of theories as to why he didn't follow her now. Perhaps he was horrified at the sight of his young daughter with an older man, or even that she had not saved herself for marriage. August Deschanel was, if nothing else, a very traditional man with traditional values. If he were still alive and found out, he'd probably show up on Mr. Evers' doorstep with some harsh words. Might even challenge him to a duel, like they used to do, in the olden days.

But he wasn't alive, and that was the problem. That was the very thing Maureen needed to flee from, as far as she could go, and Mr. Evers only lived across town, but that would have to be far enough.

Freedom wasn't always exactly as you imagined it, but when it reached for you, you reached back and didn't ask questions.

MAUREEN CHECKED HER REFLECTION IN THE OVAL mirror just inside the front door of Oak Haven. She always felt the truth of her exploits could be read in every last pore on her face, but she also knew that was the way of the guilty. The flush in her cheeks could be from anything. There was a soft breeze outside, the kind they got just before summer descended with a vengeance. She'd re-braided her hair in the backseat, while Mr. Evers checked his own guilt in the rearview mirror, leaning his neck this way and that to make sure she hadn't sucked too hard, or bitten him. She'd tried that once, and he, very seriously, told her not to do that again. When she asked why, he said he had a sensitive neck.

In these moments when Maureen stood in the foyer after a tryst with Mr. Evers, she felt as if she stood upon a precipice where her behavior remained a secret on one side and was revealed on the other. That the wrong step across the marble floor would decide things. One too many to the left, and Irish Colleen would fly from the kitchen, cheeks blazing, ready to drag Maureen by the ear and lock her in the shed. Even with blocking her thoughts, Maureen feared her siblings would find a way into her head, or that one of them, like Lizzy, might see a glimpse of the future with Maureen and Mr. Evers, and then fink to Mom and spoil the whole goddamn thing.

Each time, Maureen was frozen in place by this completely irrational, but entirely real, fear, and she knew the longer she stood, the more attention she drew to herself. When nothing happened, her fear faded to low-grade hostility, because if no one knew her secret, that also meant they didn't care enough to wonder where she'd been.

This was what it was like to live a second life, and she wondered if anyone else in the house understood this. Charles, maybe? Certainly not wretched Colleen, or that cow Madeline and her pathetic lackey, Augustus.

No, she decided. She was the only one of the seven who dared to dream beyond the prison of these four walls. The only one with the imagination, and, let's face it, the goddamn ingenuity to use what the Lord had given her to latch on to the man who would take her away from this place and into the world beyond, to a life all of her own.

Maureen stepped forward and held her breath. She squinted her eyes closed and waited. One. Two. Three. She released the breath and opened her eyes again. No screaming. No Irish Colleen demanding to know where she'd been.

Her secret was still safe.

She entered the dining room to a chaos that had nothing to do with her. Mama's admonishments passed around the table as quickly and deftly as the dishes making the rounds. Each and every one of her siblings—even Charles who had, for once, decided to join them—wore a flushed, bewildered look, one Maureen knew all too well. Just more madness, and this was never more apparent than at dinner, the only time Irish Colleen had them all in one place and could run through her litany of complaints.

Soon I'll have my own kitchen, and we'll talk about the things that interest me.

"Father always told me to defend myself," Evangeline pouted. When Maureen accepted the okra from her across the table, Evangeline's glance up revealed a split lip and some purplish darkness around her left eye. Colleen fussed at her, healing her, because it was that simple in this house. What was broken could be mended, but it was never the same. "And he hit first."

"Shit." The word was out of Maureen's mouth before she could think.

"Maureen!" came the set-your-clock-by-it reprimand from Irish Colleen.

Evangeline winked through her busted eye. Colleen chided her to be still, hissing that her magic required focus. "You should see the other guy."

"This is not a joke, Evangeline. This is your life, and I am trying my very best to guide you toward a promising future, but antics like this will send you ten steps back for every step forward!"

Maureen, feeling charitable after some time with the man who would rescue her from this place, smiled at her sister. "You're right, Evie. Daddy did say we should defend ourselves if someone hits first. Good for you."

She enjoyed the burgeoning shock spreading across her older sister's face. She could have knocked Evangeline over with a feather.

"Thanks, Maureen."

"And you're late for dinner again," Irish Colleen said from the corner of her eye, leveling a hard, if brief, look in Maureen's direction. For a fleeting moment, Maureen both worried her secret was in danger, but also felt a strange sort of warmth passing through her that her mother had bothered to notice she wasn't where she should be, when she should be.

But then it was gone, and she moved on to Elizabeth and how they might need to place her in yet another school.

Maureen tuned this out, and everything after. She thought of Peter and his tan suspenders, and those weird leather patches he wore on the elbows of his tweed jackets, like he thought he was a professor and not teaching eighth graders Shakespeare. The stupid jokes he got from the bottom of some sweet treat he enjoyed, the one Maureen could never remember the name of and didn't like the taste. Terrible jokes, really, like the one about how cannibals never ate clowns because they tasted funny. He liked to play with his uneven beard while he laughed, and he'd twirl it in his fingers like a cartoon villain, to the point it stayed that way when he was done, and he often went around the school with two inverse horns on his chin.

She smiled. While some girls daydreamed of handsome, muscled men in their Ferraris, Maureen's dreams were realistic, and thus, achievable.

Across from her, Charles cleared his throat.

Maureen looked around the table. Everyone was occupied, everyone except she and her oldest brother. When her gaze finished on him, he had his tongue rolled to the side of his mouth and he tapped his fork against his temple. Appraising her.

Are you high? she mouthed at him, because this was on par with how weird he would get when he'd been into the cocaine before coming home.

In response, Charles set his fork across the plate and folded his hands on the table, looking far more mannered than she could ever remember seeing him. His gaze didn't waver.

She wanted to ask what the hell was wrong with him, but when he didn't look away, she realized she didn't want to know. All around them, conversations flew in haphazard, diagonal directions, a lively table, as always, but not Charles. He seemed oblivious to everything else in the room, except her.

"You must all take me for a mad hen, pecking away at all of you for the sport of it," Irish Colleen was saying.

"There," Colleen said. She patted Evangeline's face, which was now devoid of any evidence of her indiscretion. Perfectly healed. The way of things, when you were a family of witches.

Maureen broke the strange locked intensity with Charles and, for once, was relieved to listen to her mother's ramblings. In that moment, she wanted nothing more.

"We don't think that, Mama," Colleen said, as she returned to the moment at hand, lacking her usual enthusiasm for authority.

"Of course *you* don't think that," Madeline said with both eyes rolled hard to the ceiling.

"I love each of you," Irish Colleen went on. Maureen was torn between sneaking glances at Charles, and the words of her mother, which had, in the moments Maureen had looked away, turned to tearful ones. "You are Deschanels. The world is yours and has been since the day of your birth."

Irish Colleen turned a pointed look on her eldest son, but he was still fixed on Maureen. Maureen felt vaguely ill, like something terrible was about to happen, something she couldn't stop. Like watching a plane crash.

"Witches. Warlocks."

All children, even Charles, turned to their mother when she spoke the words. Irish Colleen knew what her children were, but had never addressed it head-on, instead treating their abilities like afflictions, or like a drunken uncle they had to hide in an attic when guests came over.

"That's what you are, my little witches and warlocks. The world is yours, but the world is not ready for everything you have to offer. Your father left me with the tremendous burden of teaching all of you how to survive in this world being both of a very prominent, very visible family, and with a secret you can never share with anyone outside those closest to you."

She joined hands with the two children closest to her, Elizabeth and Augustus. "You think I don't understand you. That's true. But I know who you are." Her eyes traveled from one child to another. "And I love you, my little witches and warlocks. When you are angry at me, or feeling stifled by my protection, remember I would die to see you whole and well. I would give my life for any of you."

A quietness settled over the table. All seven children dropped their heads and disappeared into their own thoughts over the strange words their mother had spoken.

Irish Colleen took a sip from her wine. “We’ll be going to Ophélie for the summer. We all need a fresh start.”

A low rumble of disappointment passed around the room, but no one challenged her.

“August told me once that there was no place a Deschanel was more themselves than on the land of their ancestors.” Irish Colleen stood. “So, there we will go, and I pray this will re-center all of us and remind us what is truly important.”

SUMMER 1970

VACHERIE, LOUISIANA
NEW ORLEANS, LOUISIANA

CHAPTER 6

The Lines of Blanche and August

Ophelia Deschanel was the last of the very old ones.

Ophelia's grandfather, Charles, was the same Charles who emigrated the Deschanel family from France in 1844. The man who built Ophélie and established the Deschanels as a formidable clan in Louisiana, first as river country landowners and then as shrewd investors. The man for whom all subsequent Charleses were named, including Colleen's brother. Ophelia had seen the whole world change in her lifetime and shaped into what it became. Currently a nonagenarian, soon to be a centenarian, Ophelia had watched generations come and go; she'd guided them and sometimes worked against them, when it was necessary. But most of all, she was the only one left living who knew the full story of who they were and what happened in those turbulent early years.

The old, undying belief was that a great curse followed the family, one placed upon them by Charles' vengeful wife, Brigitte. A curse intended to thwart the prosperity of any descending from Charles, sealed with Brigitte's blood when she gave her life in the sordid act. Charles initially dismissed her dying words as insanity, until his descendants began to meet cruel and unusual ends. By the time he realized what horrors had befallen his family, there was nothing left to be done to rectify it.

The story behind Brigitte's suicide was cruel and bloody.

Charles and his family had over a decade of prosperity before the start of the Civil War. With New Orleans captured early and left mostly intact, he capitalized on this by being amenable to Union officers and their companies staying on the large property, inviting them in before they took the home for themselves. Brigitte was against this from the beginning, feeling he was a traitor to the South, but Charles insisted he was only being resourceful, and as a result of his quick-thinking, the house and most of its belongings remained in the Deschanels' possession, both during and then after the war. But this friendship with the enemy had another cost: Their only daughter, Ophélie.

While Charles drank, smoke, and gambled with the Union men by day, those same men spent their nights sneaking in and out of the poor girl's room, doing as they pleased with her. Charles either ignored her plight or approved of it, but either motivation was too egregious a sin to be borne in the eyes of Brigitte. When Ophélie ended up pregnant, someone, perhaps a soldier, perhaps Charles, perhaps even Brigitte, snuck into her room one evening and violently murdered her. Brigitte believed the sacrifice of her daughter was the cost of Charles' long list of sins and took her own life by flinging herself from the top veranda of Ophélie and onto the flagstones below. As she died, she whispered the words of her now infamous curse to Ophelia's mother, Julianne. *"There is a price. Charles and his children will pay it. As will their children, and their children, and all children who attempt to profit from anything Charles has built on the corpse of my daughter. This midnight dynasty will fall, as Ophélie fell, and there will be no more. This I promise, on my mother, and on my beloved Ophélie."*

Julianne never doubted Brigitte's words would bear out as true, nor did her daughter, Ophelia. Ophelia never had children of her own, but she passed this belief to her brother, Charles', two children, August and Blanche, and later, to August's children.

Only some of the present day Deschanels believed in the family curse. Colleen believed it, because Ophelia believed it, and not a single person in this family, past or present, had lived as long as she had. Ophelia said she'd only lived that long because she never married, and as a woman could not further the heir's line. Colleen wasn't sure if that was true, but she was grateful her great-aunt had lived long enough to pass down to her the story of the foundation of who they were.

Whether she believed it or not, Colleen decided having children wasn't worth the risk. When she told Irish Colleen she never planned to start a family, her mother had just accused her of *listening to that old coot* again and dismissed her.

Colleen believed Ophelia believed, and that was enough. It was the biggest and most important thing the family still had, the faith of this loyal old woman.

The one and only thing Ophelia did not seem to know was how and when the Deschanels came into possession of their rare abilities. She only knew it all started in France, many years before the family came to Louisiana. One day, she said, someone would connect all the right dots and put the story together.

COLLEEN LIVED DAILY WITH THE FEAR SHE MIGHT GET the call her great-aunt had died. It was an inevitability of living to such an age, and at ninety-two, it didn't take any serious illness. A cold, a short fever. A fall. Ophelia had first lived out her twilight years with her niece, Blanche, but Blanche was only a few short years from seventy herself, and already some members of her family were trying to oust her from her own manor, Femme Forte, claiming she no longer possessed the faculties to manage it herself. Blanche, having had children from two of her three marriages, often had something akin to turf wars when it came to Femme Forte, though everyone knew it would go to Eugenia Fontenot, the eldest from her favorite marriage.

Irish Colleen had offered Ophelia a room in their home many

times. August had enjoyed a very close relationship with this aunt, and, had he lived, would have made the same offer. But Ophelia was as stubborn as she was wise and proclaimed that children needed sunshine to thrive, not dust and cobwebs. Irish Colleen hadn't understood that, but Colleen thought maybe she did. She hadn't been at all surprised when Ophelia up and moved into The Gardens all by herself, to the distress of everyone else.

While Ophelia had always placed great importance in sharing these tales of who they were and where they'd come from, she emphasized even more the need for the family to open their arms wide to the future, not the past. *The past informs us; in showing us how we got here, it informs us how not to do it all again,* Ophelia liked to say. *The future is our blueprint. We must follow it as far from the past as we can.*

When Ophelia asked Colleen to take the empty Council seat, Colleen was beside herself. She may only be the third born in the heir's line, but she took the responsibility of her family with the gravity it deserved. As some of the older ones died off, Ophelia did not start with the next oldest. Instead, she said this new generation was the future, and she must have time with them, to shape them, instruct them, help them lead, before she gave up the ghost and surrendered to the eternal sleep.

Not counting Ophelia, the oldest of the seven Council members was Pierce Guidry, at forty-four. Eugenia Fontenot was thirty, and Cassius Broussard was turning twenty-eight. All three were Blanche's children.

The rest of the Council were younger still. Pierce's daughters, Pansy and Kitty, were twenty-one and sixteen. Colleen, at eighteen, was the only representative from the heir's line. When Ophelia finally retired—Colleen, though practical about many things, refused to use the other word—Colleen would look to her siblings for the next member of the Council. There were too many from Blanche's line. August's line needed better representation.

Evangeline, she thought, was the most likely candidate. Charles had no care for any of this, and Augustus had priorities that did not involve sitting in dusty chambers discussing the matters of witches and warlocks.

This was a refrain at almost any family reunion, which inevitably revealed new faces each time. *Are you from the line of Blanche or August?* The answer was often obvious before it came, for the line of August was only his seven children, and the line of Blanche was preparing for great-grandchildren. Guidry, Fontenot, Broussard, these names were as authentic and respected as Deschanel, because everyone knew Miss Blanche had replenished the family after all the great tragedies had thinned the line. Blanche had started building her dynasty as soon as she was old enough to leave home. August did not have his first child until he was forty-five.

Ophelia liked to tell Colleen, as they strolled through the endless rows of exotic flora of The Gardens, that none of this was important. Whether of Blanche or August, all interests were intertwined. The flourishment of the family should be important to everyone sharing their blood, and if Blanche's line held the lion's share of seats, what of it? When the seven had their children, the dynamics would shift.

Colleen thought of this as she sat with her great-aunt in the parlor adjoining the Collective chambers. It was past two, and Colleen needed to start the long drive back to Vacherie, to Ophélie, soon, or she might fall asleep at the wheel. But her mind was troubled, and so she'd stayed after the Council meeting in hopes some wisdom from Ophelia would settle her.

"You carry the burden of them all," Ophelia observed. Her tea sloshed against the sides of the mug as her shaking hands drew it slowly to her wrinkled mouth. "Do you not ever wonder, my dearest Colleen, why we take on jobs no one ever asked us to do?"

"What do you mean?" Colleen wanted to reach forward and steady the cup for her great-aunt, but to do so would be offensive.

"You are not Charles," Ophelia said through her slow, languid drawl, like gravel stretching across silk. "Is it not his responsibility, as the heir?"

"Pardon me, Tante Ophelia, I'm not sure if the question is rhetorical or not," Colleen said with a frown. "If I waited for Charles to do as everyone expects, I'd carry my disappointment to the grave, I'm afraid."

Ophelia's mouth twitched. It was almost a smile. "Charles is who he is. And his children..." A racking cough pitched through her, cutting off her words. "I must remember myself! I cannot go around sharing the future as if it is mine to dole out."

"What about Charles' children?"

Ophelia waved a trembling hand through the air. "Neither here. Neither there. That is tomorrow, and we are in today. People rarely change in any meaningful way, Colleen. This is not soothsaying, this is a fact of human nature. I know what troubles you."

"You do?"

"Why, everything, of course."

Colleen's laugh was tinged with exhaustion. "You know me well, Tante."

"I know you well, because you are so much like me. You are who my daughter would have been, had I chosen the boon of motherhood. I have carried this burden, Colleen, all my life. Blanche and August wanted little to do with who we were, but their children... their children, and their grandchildren, they know. They believe. And when I'm gone—"

"Stop," Colleen said. "You're perfectly healthy."

"I'm way past empty platitudes. I am old and gnarled, like the oaks lining this great mansion. In you, I see my work as complete." Her arm, that thin vellum of the very old, covered in bluish lines and darkening spots, reached forward and offered a light pat to Colleen's leg. A cough overtook her again. She drew it back, shaking. "But it is a lonely burden, Colleen. Do you know of the Serenity prayer, my dear?"

Colleen nodded. She wanted to cry, but she didn't understand why.

"Recite it to me."

Colleen ran her hands over her jeans. The lump in her throat, the one she had in almost every conversation with her beloved aunt, caused her voice to crack. She cleared her throat. "God grant me the serenity to accept the things I cannot change, the courage to change the things I can, and—"

"The wisdom to know the difference," Ophelia finished with her. "This burden cannot be borne if you are unable to separate those people and circumstances you can affect and that you cannot. You stayed tonight because you are worried about your siblings."

Colleen bowed her head to hide the tears forming. "Yes."

"They grow weary of your maturity. They wish you would be their sister, not their authority."

"They don't understand how much I wish I could let it all go, too."

"Well, you can let it go. Of course you can." Ophelia began the slow task of reaching again for her tea. "They do."

"But—"

"Yes, but," Ophelia replied. "But someone has to do it, is that what you were about to tell me? Someone has to carry the torch? Lead the family?"

"I suppose, yes."

"I won't argue with that." Tea dribbled down her chin as she took a shaking sip. "My father, Jean, had no interest in it. Nor did my brother, Charles, and then his children—your father, your aunt Blanche—failed to fully appreciate the task. It has always fallen to me, a second born, a woman without issue, without a true home. Your road will be different, Colleen. You will feel alone at times, but that is not because you will be. You have a boyfriend. Rory. How is that going for you?"

Colleen leaned back and shrugged. "I don't know, to be honest. I care dearly for Rory. He's one of my oldest friends, and I feel safe around him."

"Feeling safe with an outsider is not to be taken lightly. Not all Deschanels will find that."

"The Sullivans are practically family."

Ophelia grinned. "Go on."

"I am so torn between how I feel for him and what I know lies ahead for me. Rory has his life picked out for him already. Since he was a boy, he's known he would go to law school and join the rest of his family at the firm. I suppose I've always known I wanted to go to medical school, but it's different."

"Tell me how it's different," Ophelia said, though her patient eyes conveyed she already knew the answer and only wanted to hear Colleen say it.

"There's a difference between a dream and an expectation. Rory will make a fine lawyer, I'm sure of it. He's a good man, with strong convictions. But he has never, not once that I know of, thought of doing something different. It never occurred to him to be anything but what the rest of his family is. I want to be the first surgeon in the Deschanel family. I don't want to stay in New Orleans for graduate school, and go to Tulane, where everyone else goes, because it's easy, or the norm. Once I have my degree in hand, I want to go to Scotland, or Paris, and finish my education elsewhere, so when I come back I have more to offer my family than just my heritage. I don't want the same wheels to spin us around and around until we keep returning to where we are."

"That is a very astute consideration," Ophelia said after a pause. "Could Rory not fit into this?"

"Does he have to?"

Ophelia drew her shawl tighter around her. Though the sweltering heat and humidity was at its peak, even in the late evenings, she was often overtaken with bouts of the chills. "Would you like to know if he is in your future? I can divine this for you. I could tell you who you will marry, what your children will be like. Your joys. Your sorrows. Some do better never knowing... others, like us, find comfort in preparation."

Colleen stared at her. She had always known, of course, that Ophelia could do this, but had never considered she might be given such an offer. To know what the future held... yes, this could give her comfort. It could help her to know if her efforts with her siblings would ever bear fruit, would help to know if pushing Rory away or letting him in was the right way. Colleen feared the unknown, because it was beyond her control, and what she could not control had the potential to harm her.

But to possess such knowledge took away the gift of making mistakes and learning from them. It dulled the joys and sharpened the losses. There was gain, yes, but she would surrender so much more, if she knew what her life would be like in five, ten, fifty years. And if she saw something terrible, she would live her life in dread of that moment and would forget to live.

"No, thank you, Tante. I think it's better to take my chances and see where the future takes me."

Ophelia nodded. "I would not have accepted such a gift, either, despite my pragmatism. But I offer it from a place of love. There will be a time when I cannot give you this gift again."

"I know."

"Your sister, Elizabeth. She inherited this, as well, and it is slowly driving her to madness."

Colleen breathed out. "I know. I don't know how to help her."

"You cannot," Ophelia replied and then shook her head. "Forgive me, Colleen, for that was both wisdom *and* divination, and you only asked for the former."

COLLEEN ARRIVED AT THE OLD PLANTATION HOUSE A quarter after three in the morning. The massive structure, with its forty-five rooms and three stories, with its central hall and massive cypress parlors and twinkling chandeliers, was big and lonely, even with the eight of them living there for the summer. August and Blanche had grown up in this monstrous home, and so had their ancestors. August refused to raise his own family in such isolation, and when he married Irish Colleen, he promptly relocated the Deschanels to New Orleans.

The Greek Revival mansion hummed with old life, with a dozen clocks and with the fauna holding courts outside. Each step she took through the central hall set off a new chain of sounds, which echoed through the emptiness.

Was this an example of appreciating their past without embracing it? Ophelia said this place was haunted not only with the ghosts of their ancestors, but also the weight of decisions made. The old office on the third floor had seen many deals brokered, some of which benefitted the family today. The faint perfume of cigars from generations past still lived in the old wood; behind the lightly peeling red and gold wallpaper of the parlors.

Richard, their butler, peeked his head out from behind the bannister, coming from the direction of the west kitchen. "You okay, Miss Colleen?"

"Yes, Richard, I'm fine. Why are you still up?"

"Why, Miss Colleen, I've always waited up for our family's Council members. Least, that is, when we had them in the heir's line."

Colleen watched him hover protectively in the shadows. Richard and his sister, Condoleezza, were as much, no more, a staple of Ophélie as the deep heritage whispered in the foundation. They were close to retiring but never would, they said. They'd been raised here, almost as a sibling of August, and the family rumors said that they *were* his siblings, illegitimate children of the known libertine Charles II. If true, and at this point they were less rumors than casual fact, this made the two of them Colleen's aunt and uncle.

"I'm home now, so no need to worry anymore."

"I never worry about you."

She kissed his cheek and made her way up the first set of steep, half-carpeted steps. The edges of the fabric frayed from years of use, and she wondered if anyone would ever live here full-time again, would ever tend to these details.

It would not be her. She knew that much.

She was close to passing out on the spot but had an urge to be near someone. With most of her siblings not speaking to her, she considered whether any of them would give her the comfort she sought.

Colleen stopped at Evangeline's room. She peeked inside. Her sister was sleeping half-on, half-off the half-tester bed. Colleen crept in and eased Evangeline back into place. Evangeline stirred, and Colleen slid in beside her.

But even this bond was fractured. With her relationship with Rory neatly defined as more than friendship, Evangeline had pulled back, as if sensing something had shifted, something that left her out of things.

Evangeline woke. Her eyes hung half-open, drawn back to her interrupted sleep.

She turned her back to Colleen and settled back into the bed. Not a rejection, but not an invitation, either.

Colleen curled into her sister and wondered if things would ever be okay again.

CHAPTER 7

Fire & Rain

Madeline had trouble piecing together exactly what had happened. How it had all gone so horribly wrong, so quickly. Even after the drugs and excitement of the day wore off, the picture was hazy, full of emotions but devoid on details.

To her left, Augustus drove without words. His hands rolled over the leather wheel, knuckles white. He adjusted his set jaw every few seconds or so, and each time she thought he was about to speak, but he never did. His silence said everything he didn't.

Armstrong Park. Congo Square. Madeline had secretly attended several protests there over the past year, but she felt connected to the land for other reasons. The true ancestors of New Orleans—not the wealthy landowners, not the entitled white barons, not the Deschanels—were those who had built it; literally died toiling in the sub-tropical sun as their own rights were stripped away to boost the privilege of others. Congo Square was their place, where they went to feel human again, and to connect with their culture; where they were unafraid and uninhibited. Where the Second line was born, and all that beautiful, magical jazz and blues, and so many dances.

There were few things in the world more awful to Madeline than how everyone in New Orleans, from the teachers to even her own family, had painted over those days of slavery with a lily-white brush. "Times were different then." Oh, how many times had she wanted to slap those words from the mouths of someone in authority? As if any words could erase such barbaric, inhuman actions. When Madeline stood on the bricks in Congo Square, she was drawn to the reality of the past, and though it was painful, she would never shy away from this. Just as she would never stop trying to end the war, which was just another form of slavery, as she saw it, or genocides across the world *still happening*. Still! Her teachers might disappear into the comfort that they were in "different times," but the world hadn't changed much at all, not really.

This, all of this, brought out the best and worst of Madeline, and whenever she stood upon those old bricks, she was filled with a fierce and powerful need to correct the wrongs of the world still present. She could not change the past. She could correct those trying to rewrite it, but she couldn't rescind the wrongs done. But, unlike those who preferred to live in their comfortable homes and never think of such "unpleasant things," Madeline promised herself she would never forget, and she would take these lessons seriously. The past informed the future. The past was cyclical. It was Augustus who had said these things to her, likely without knowing how she would apply them and turn them into her personal mantra.

And now he wasn't speaking to her. She'd never seen him mad enough to ignore her, so the truth of that evening must be even more terrible than she thought.

Jill and Josh. They'd picked her up in Josh's ugly orange van with the shag carpet that had dozens of burned out spots from how clumsy Jill was with her joints. Madeline never liked sitting in the back, because she knew smoking grass wasn't the only thing they did excessively there. She knew because she'd slept with Josh back there herself, once upon a time, or many times. Before Jill... before Madeline realized his interest in protests and activism was more about the thrill than the conscience. She always sat at the far end of the bench, nestling herself behind the peeling leather of the driver's bucket seat, and tried to keep her eyes forward.

. . .

Augustus asked her how she could hang out with friends who didn't share her passionate beliefs, but it wasn't so simple for Madeline. Even those who believed activism was a calling still went home to their suburban lives and nothing changed. They could turn it off, and on, as needed, and Madeline could not. As an empath, she had to learn to accept that to function in the world, and so she accepted that her friends were a means to an end. If Josh and Jill were going to the protest, she would go with them. Their motivations were less important to her than having a safe ride. Hitchhiking was a dangerous business in New Orleans, and even in Madeline's most erratic moods, she knew better.

The National Guard had formed a line in their riot gear. Madeline remembered that much. They were there when Madeline and her friends showed up, ready. She also remembered thinking that you didn't wear riot gear unless you were expecting, or hoping for, a riot. She liked to stand in front of these lines sometimes and inspect the faces behind the heavy bulletproof plastic shields. How many of them wished they were out there protesting with the other hippies? How many of them ached for one single excuse to open fire, like they had at Kent State?

Chanting and signs everywhere. Madeline had brought a sign the first time, but she felt they impeded her and wore down her energy. But oh, how their words inspired her and connected her to them. She recognized a few faces, but most were complete strangers, united by their common disgust for the governments of the world.

I don't give a damn for Uncle Sam.

Heil Nixon.

Bombing for peace is like fucking for virginity.

Cajuns against the war.

We love the Beatles!

Madeline had smoked half a joint on the ride over, so she was feeling fine by the time they settled into a spot on the square. The air was a cloud of smoke, daring the authorities. But they were too serious and too busy looking scary and official in their heavy gear.

"I'M NOT TELLING MOM." AUGUSTUS' LOW, disappointed voice pulled Madeline from her reconstruction of the night.

She didn't think he would, because he never did, but the way he said it provoked the question. "Why not?"

"For her sake, not yours. She's had enough heartbreak," her brother answered, and then his face returned to the same pensive detachment as he navigated the car down River Road.

Madeline could weather all the bullshit her siblings and mother could dish out, but her brother's disappoint was too sharp a cut.

SHE RETURNED TO THE DAY, SEARCHING FOR THE moment.

Was it after the second joint? It hit her harder than the first, and in a much different way. Time became fluid, and the world had no fixed axis, no stability. She wavered on her feet as the chants came from deep within her. When her vision blurred, she reached for Jill, but Jill was dancing several feet away, caught in a moment with herself.

"What was in that?" Madeline asked, for she knew by now this was no standard grass.

"Angel dust, angel," Josh said, followed by that annoying stoner laugh that had been at least part of why she broke things off with him.

"Why didn't you tell me?"

He swayed to the sounds of Crosby, Stills, & Nash rolling off a nearby portable radio. With a grin, he pulled down his ridiculous John Lennon glasses and winked. "Feels good, doesn't it?"

"Feels like someone lied to me," Madeline said, and that was the last she remembered seeing Josh or Jill.

. . .

AUGUSTUS PULLED BEHIND THEIR HOUSE AND PARKED next to the other cars. Madeline sighed and reached for the door, but when he made no move to do the same, she withdrew her arm and sat back against the seat.

"I don't get it," he said. "What happened?"

"I don't know," Madeline said, and she hated how true this was.

"You know, I promised myself I wouldn't ever use my powers of persuasion to get our family out of trouble. It's unethical. It's... wrong." Augustus rested his head on his hands, which still gripped the wheel. "It's wrong, Madeline, but I did it, to protect you, and I thought I would feel good about this, but all I feel is sick."

"I don't want you to feel that way," she said, helpless, trying to remember.

"It's too late, Maddy."

SOMEONE THREW THEIR SIGN AT THE NATIONAL GUARD. It missed, or perhaps ricocheted off a shield, Madeline wasn't sure. Her head was a mess of disorganized chaos, and though she searched for a thread, anything to help her find her grounding again, she only spun further away from anything tangible and real.

From there, a movement started, and signs flew from the crowd and into a growing pile of wood and words. Madeline watched in confused wonder as they flew over her head, beside her, across the square. Why were they throwing their signs? She didn't understand. And the guards... they stood motionless, waiting. Like a lion watching a gazelle with the measured patience of one who knows the reward is worth the wait. As if they knew something was coming and were biding their time.

Someone yelled out, "Light it up! Light it up!" Madeline brightened at the strange suggestion, which seemed perfectly reasonable and also... also.... she lost her thought process as she stumbled through the excited crowd, but then found it once more. Light it up. Yes, she could do that.

No one knew that, of course. Not her mother. Not Augustus. Certainly not all the weird people gathered around a pile of signs. Madeline couldn't just be born with one strange and terrible affliction. No, she also had to be an elementalist. Fire. She could create it, with only a channeled focus from her mind. Conjure it from nothing.

"Light it up, light it up!"

"Why did you start a fire? That's what I don't get." Augustus shook his head without looking at her. He hadn't looked at her once. "I don't get it, Madeline. You're not like this. You protect, you don't destroy. Isn't that the whole point of protest? To make the world better?"

"I hate when you call me Madeline."

"I hate when you set an entire park on fire and I have to brainwash everyone to keep you out of prison."

The pile of signs was a bonfire in seconds. Not a gradual burn, but a whoosh of flame that momentarily silenced the crowd. When they found their words, the questions started. Who had done that? No one, not one person had been seen to walk up to the pile. It was as if they'd spontaneously combusted from the sheer will of the chanting alone.

But someone had seen something. Someone from the National Guard had witnessed Madeline, head pointed to the sky in her strange trip, hands working through the air like a mad witch. She was pulled from her reverie when her face slammed into the bricks. Blood filled her mouth. Confusion set in.

Fire. A fire. She'd started a fire. Yes, light it up, light it up! Light it up for....

For what?

Hands, all over her back. Her wrists burned as metal tightened. Her mouth was a sea of copper. Now, the chanting was directed at her, to free her, to let her go. They couldn't have known what she'd done, but they were collectively against the authorities in every way. She could have done murder and they'd still be chanting for her freedom, because their common enemy exonerated them from any real wrongdoing.

The earth spun in wild circles as they yanked her to her feet. What had happened? It all came so fast. The flames. The assault. Now, the fire stretched into the trees and the sky was a beautiful dance of red and gold. Madeline only had a second to admire the peculiar beauty of this violent destruction before she was dragged through the square, her feet scrambling to keep up and find purchase.

"You have the right to remain silent."

Silent. No. She hadn't come here to be silent. Madeline could never be silent.

"You resisted arrest."

"I resisted, period. That's what I do, Aggie. I resist." The headache piercing her skull was unbelievable. She wished she could just ask Colleen or Evie to heal it away, but that would mean making peace, and she had nothing to say to either of them. "Do you realize... have you ever stopped to realize, to consider, that you and Charles will *never* see a day of battle, never serve, because of who you are? That Mama will never have to receive your casket with the flag draped over it in mourning?"

"Stop changing the subject."

"This *is* the subject. It's the whole subject. None of us are equal until all of us are equal, and right now our president is leading the less fortunate men of this nation to sacrifice because he sees the loss of those less fortunate men as an acceptable one to achieve his own personal aims!"

"I support you," Augustus said, his voice throbbing through her head, "because I know your heart is in the right place. Because what you do is peaceful. Burning down half of Armstrong Park is *not* peaceful. It's degenerate behavior, and I just don't get it."

"You never have. You pretend to, for my sake I suppose, but you don't get it."

"I'm not going to be around as much soon," he said. Everything about her brother seemed strained. "I've filed the paperwork to start my business. Once everything falls into place, that's where my focus will have to be."

"Are you saying I'm not your problem anymore?" She wanted to be excited for him, but found she couldn't, even though her selfishness was terrible in the face of all he'd done for her.

"You've never been my problem. I love you, and I don't want to lose you to your choices." He sighed. "I worry without me to push you that you might…"

He didn't finish.

AUGUSTUS HAD BEEN HER CALL FROM THE POLICE station, naturally. There wasn't anyone else. At the moment she'd called him, she had almost no recollection of the events that had brought her there. She didn't remember the fire. Didn't know, then, that the charges pending against her were so severe they had to wait for the judge to set bail.

She'd sat in the cold plastic chair while Augustus calmly spoke to the officers. It all looked so reasonable, and congenial, from where she sat, but then she saw her brother's stance change. Whenever he needed to employ his particular brand of magic, he always squared up, like a pugilist falling into formation. It was subtle, unless you knew what to look for, and Madeline recognized it immediately.

It was over so fast, she could hardly believe everything Augustus said when she first jumped into the front seat. Her head spun and spun, half from the drugs, half from his words. *They were going to charge you with felony arson. Arson, Madeline. Multiple counts. The kind of charge that would keep you out of a good college, or any decent job. Do you understand?*

No, she hadn't. Not then. But she did now. She remembered it all.

She could explain this. Josh had laced her grass with a hallucinogen, and then everything went so wildly out of her control, and...

Madeline stopped herself. She had disappointed her brother, herself, and the cause.

"I'm sorry," she said simply.

Augustus' expression twitched. He cast a half-look in her direction and then slid out of the car, heading into the house without her.

WHILE HER OLDER SISTER WAS BURNING DOWN NEW Orleans, Maureen surrendered to the demands of the lover who would take her away from all her suffering.

He'd always wanted to make love in water, he said, which sounded borderline ludicrous, if not pointless, but Maureen had a strong self-interest in keeping him happy, so she acquiesced. Even pretended to be into it, which only pushed him over the edge, until he was driving to the south shore of Lake Pontchartrain, to where he said he knew of just the spot.

When he stripped down to nothing, Maureen was skeptical. Even in the summer, the lake wasn't exactly a sauna, and her skin prickled with gooseflesh just thinking about it. She couldn't use the excuse she had to be home, because she was only in New Orleans to "spend the night at Maria's," and her mother wouldn't be expecting her back at Ophélie until tomorrow. But Mr. Evers—Peter—was so insistent in his beckoning that she had no time for more than coquettish protests.

He held her with one arm and the dock with another. The water wasn't as cold as she thought, but she had chills nonetheless, thinking of how exposed they both were. Her back pressed into the wood piling as Peter began his fevered lovemaking. Maureen smiled and moaned in all the right places, but her mind was elsewhere.

She saw herself in his kitchen. She hadn't been in many kitchens, so this was the kitchen from *Bewitched,* which was her favorite show because she could appreciate irony from time to time. Maureen wore a pink apron with frilly lace, because pink was her color, and the smells coming from the kitchen would send any man into spasms of joy. In this fantasy, Maureen was a phenomenal cook, which of course she would need to work on in real life because she had turned away any attempts at learning from her mother.

Peter came up behind her, wrapping his arms around her tiny waist. He asked her what smelled so amazing, then made a joke about how the food smelled great, too. She laughed, kissed him. Everything was so wonderful. She couldn't imagine being happier. Except... she had news for him. Huge, wonderful, important news. *I'm pregnant, darling.*

His shuddering orgasm pulled her back to the strange, cold moment in the still water of the Pontchartrain.

CHAPTER 8

You Stupid Girl

Jared said he had something for him.

Charles tensed as he sat in his car, waiting. He rolled his hands over the wheel, squeezing, releasing. An unlit cigarette dangled from his lips, waiting to be useful. A part of him thought Rory had to be full of shit. No way was Maureen involved in trouble. The girl wasn't clever enough to tie her shoes on the first try. It was highly unlikely she'd been hiding anything from anyone.

But Jared said he had something, and that he wasn't comfortable sharing over the phone. Jared was a conspiracy theorist who assumed the government was always watching and listening. Though utterly ridiculous, it nonetheless left Charles feeling ill. If Jared thought whatever news he had to share was serious enough to put on his tinfoil hat, then it *was* serious.

Charles lit the cigarette and inhaled a lungful of calming smoke. He released it into the warm car and rolled his head over the seat back.

Maureen, you stupid, stupid girl. What have you done?

Jared checked the area extensively before sliding into Charles' passenger seat. Charles had the keen urge to smack him over the head, but he needed the information first, and he was already well past the point of losing his patience. Jared was twenty minutes late.

"Where the fuck have you been?"

Jared gripped the folder like a man holding another man's death sentence. "I took a longer route to make sure I wasn't being followed."

"Why the fuck would—" Charles forcibly stopped himself. The information first. "I don't have a lot of time," he lied. "What do you have?"

"Well," Jared said, and Charles had a suspicion the dude was going to draw this out for effect, "Maureen is definitely involved with someone."

"Who?"

"A man."

"Jesus Christ, Jared, *who*?"

Jared again checked the exterior perimeter. Charles thought to himself that he really might become a murderer before this encounter came to an end.

"My sources say their little tryst has been going on since before the last school year ended."

"Jared, if you don't tell me..." Charles frowned as a thought silenced his words. "Wait, did you say *man*?"

Jared closed his eyes and drew in a dramatic breath. He slowly handed over the folder. "Peter Evers. As in—"

Charles ripped the folder open. "Mr. Evers? That middle school idiot who taught Dickens or some shit?" He laughed. "Nah, man, there's no way. There. Is. No. Way."

"Shakespeare," Jared corrected solemnly, "and there is. Halfway through the stack, you will find Exhibit C."

"Exhibit what the fuck?"

"The pictures, Charles." Jared was clearly annoyed at his lack of enthusiasm for the details he'd lovingly prepared.

Charles threw one discarded page after another into the back seat as he shuffled through meaningless paperwork. When he got to the first of the grainy black and white photos, shoddily developed in the high school lab, it looked like, he stopped breathing.

Maureen, sitting atop her English teacher in the backseat of his beat-up sports car.

Maureen, pressed into the pilings of a dock by the flabby frame of Mr. Evers.

Maureen, kissing Mr. Evers behind a building.

Maureen. Maureen. Maureen.

"This man taught me. Taught all of us."

"I was in one of his classes, too," Jared added, as if Charles gave a shit.

Charles slammed back into his seat. His mind was overloaded with all he'd seen, and with the budding rage clouding those thoughts with new ones. This man... this *teacher*... was a criminal, and he had chosen the wrong girl to practice his sick perversions on.

"Hey, Charles, I was thinking... I've got tickets to Jethro Tull at The Warehouse tonight. You in?"

"You're still here?"

Jared flashed him an appropriately pathetic look. "Why wouldn't I be?"

"Do I need to answer that?"

Jared paused, as if waiting for Charles to say he was joking. When that didn't happen, he sighed and opened the door. Before stepping out, he said, "Should I stay on her?"

Charles set the pictures down to his lap. He ground his teeth together, a small grunt escaping. "No, and if I hear about this from *anyone,* anyone at all, even some random starving kid someone adopted in rural Africa, I'll come for *your* nuts, turn around, and feed them to those same starving kids."

"Hey, now—"

Charles threw the car into reverse and peeled through the gravel. Jared jumped back as the door flapped in the wind, and though Charles didn't look in his rearview, he knew the dolt was still standing and watching, dumbfounded.

He stretched across the passenger seat and pulled the door closed.

COLLEEN KNEW SHE WAS SUPPOSED TO ENJOY SEX. SHE knew this because she had a strong clinical understanding of all the body's responses, and the response to sexual stimulation was one of the most powerful and most unique. Sex had literally started wars, ended careers, and offered the one who was desired a power and advantage unlike any other.

She did enjoy it, to an extent. Rory never rushed; was always attentive to her needs, which even she didn't quite have a hold on yet. He always checked to see if she was enjoying herself, and she had learned to sometimes fake this, for his sake, for any disinterest on her part wasn't his fault. Her mind was simply too full to invite in anyone, or anything, else. Her intellectual mind knew she should not only be having a great time whenever she was with Rory, but that she was fortunate to have such a tender and mindful lover.

But her intellectual mind was the problem. She could not turn it off, not for a minute. She loved Rory, in her own way, even if it was not the same way he loved her. But Colleen had always seen the path she wanted and had followed it. No man would change that. Even her dedication to her siblings couldn't change that.

Yet Rory viewed their union as a pivotal shift in their lives that warranted compromise. He lay at her side after they made love, one hand lazily stroking her hair as the other animatedly swept through the air with his proclamations of the plans they'd make. They were both going to Tulane for their undergraduate studies, so they didn't have to break up or attempt a long-distance relationship. That gave them time to pick a graduate school together, too, where they could attend jointly. By the time they were done, they could have their nice wedding and begin planning their family. Two kids, he said he wanted, though he would welcome a third if God intended it, or if Colleen really wanted more.

He never stopped for her approval, only to see if she was tracking. Rory wasn't an innately selfish person, so she interpreted his lack of concern for her feelings more as him misreading her own interest in the plans he proposed. He simply couldn't imagine she didn't see the potential in what they had, as he did. And so she smiled and kissed him back, unsure how to tell him she was mostly indifferent to where things were going, while her mind wandered to those things more pressing to her.

They'd been at Ophélie a month now, even Charles and Augustus who could have gone anywhere. Irish Colleen allowed Rory to stay over now that Colleen was eighteen, but Colleen almost wished her mother hadn't permitted it, so she had an excuse to be alone and think.

Ophélie was the home of their ancestors, and Colleen felt most connected to her heritage when she walked the long cypress boards and ate from the china purchased by her great-great-grandmother. Irish Colleen took this a step further, believing it had restorative properties for her children, though she never gave a reasonable explanation for how this could be possible. And Colleen had only seen everyone, herself included, struggle this summer.

Elizabeth's visions were stronger now, and she rarely emerged from her room outside of mealtimes. Maureen walked around with a strange grin and a dazed demeanor, one that made Colleen think they might have a problem on their hands. Evangeline had pulled away since Colleen had been dating Rory, or whatever it was they were doing, and nothing Colleen could do would sway Evangeline into spending time with her, not even the reminder that college would take up more of her time.

Madeline, though, she was the worst of all. Coming and going at all hours, locking herself in her room when she was home. Hunger strikes had become the norm, and the strong smell of marijuana wafted from under the old door to her room every night. Then, the other night, she'd come in past midnight with Augustus, who was plainly furious with her. Augustus was never angry with Madeline, so what could that mean?

Rory had rolled atop her and was making earnest efforts to gain her interest in some foreplay. Colleen played along, but as usual, her heart wasn't in it. She could never surrender to her own happiness when others suffered.

"Goddammit, Sullivan, get the fuck off my sister!"

Colleen had never seen Rory move so fast. He held tight to the blanket as he scrambled to the other side of the room. Colleen tugged her sweater back down over her stomach and glared at her brother. "You need to learn to knock, Huck!"

"This is my fucking plantation, and I'll do as I please."

"Say that to Mother," Colleen retorted.

"We have bigger issues. In fact, we have one very big fucking issue, Colleen."

"I should go," Rory said as he searched around for his trousers.

"You think?" Charles snapped.

"I'll call you later," Colleen said, because that was the sort of thing people said. She sighed. "I'm sorry about my brother."

"Don't apologize for me, when I don't mean it," Charles said with a heavy smirk. As Rory gathered his backpack and went to move past him, Charles puffed out his chest with a tight jerk, like he was challenging him to a cock fight.

Rory waved from behind Charles and ran out the door.

"What a fucking dolt," Charles said with a thumb behind him. "Are you decent? If I sit on the bed, am I gonna regret it?"

Colleen threw her blanket aside. "I'll accept your apology whenever. While you're at it, apologize to Rory, too."

"Yeah, right." Charles laughed. He tugged at the collar of his button-down shirt. "Maureen is in some deep shit, Colleen. Like waist-deep and sinking fast."

She crossed her arms and leaned into the heavy frame of the bed. "Oh? And you suddenly care what she's up to?"

"She's fucking her middle school English teacher. I sure as shit care about *that.*"

The room went utterly still and cold, and Colleen couldn't have moved if she tried. "No. That's not... which one?" She shook her head. "No, that can't be right."

"Mr. Evers. That middle-aged fuck who drives the old Camaro he can't afford to fix up, and has a beer belly the size of a regulation basketball."

"Mr. Evers? The man is married. He has kids."

Charles threw his hands up. "And he's sticking his dick in our sister."

"Why does everything have to be so vulgar with you?"

"He's had our sister in the Biblical way. Many times. Better?"

"Let's back up." Colleen's mouth was a bed of cotton. Her heart had picked up to such a pace she knew she needed to measure out her breathing or she'd be in a full-blown panic soon. "How do you know this?"

"I have my ways."

"Not good enough, Huck. Not for this."

He heaved a large sigh. "I had one of my fuckwit lackeys follow her for a month. The evidence is real, Leena. I'm not making this up. There are fucking *pictures* of this pedophile *fu*—having carnal relations with our Maureen."

"Okay." Colleen closed her eyes and focused on her breathing. Steady. In. Out. "Okay, let's think."

"Think?" Charles shot up off the bed. "I *think* I'm going to murder this perverted fuck, is that what you meant?"

"Don't even joke about something like that," Colleen hissed. "Before we do anything, we need to talk to Maureen."

"And say what? She's going to deny it."

"Of course she is, but if we show her she's safe with us, that we can help her through this. We can help her, come up with a plan."

"Oh, for Christ's sake, Colleen, she's not the least bit rational. If she has a brain cell not devoted to this motherfucker, it's probably wasted on cotton candy and those weird little balls on her sweaters. This is *Maureen* we're talking about, not Evangeline, not Madeline. She only knows what she wants, and if we tell her she can't have it, she's going to want it more. If that happens, who knows what she might do?"

Charles' words gave Colleen pause. She thought, maybe, he was speaking from his own experience, and that made sense, for if Maureen was like anyone in the family, it was Charles. It was also the only wisdom she'd heard from him... maybe ever. If he was espousing wisdom, he wasn't out acting irrational and getting himself in trouble. "Maybe you're right. Then what do you suggest?"

"We could get Augustus to talk to her. Convince her she hates the guy."

Colleen shook her head. "No, we have always promised in our family never to use magic against one another, not without consent. I won't break that rule. Not even for this."

She expected Charles to argue, but he only nodded. "Maybe we can get Mama to send her away to boarding school."

"No," Colleen said. "When this all comes out in the open, we will need her here, so we can look after her."

"Right." Charles pressed his palms to his temples. "Let's get Augustus. He always knows what to do."

Colleen found this curious, how Charles was so unlike his brother but often sought him out when he needed guidance. She balked at the notion that hers wasn't enough, but also realized the more heads they had in solving this, the better they could support their sister.

"He'll be home in a couple hours. Mini family meeting?"

Charles smacked her shoulder. "Great. Grab her. I'll meet you downstairs in a couple hours."

"Where are you going?"

"Out."

CHAPTER 9

It Only Stops When it Hits the Wall

Madeline rifled through the drawers in her mother's bedroom with only a moderate sense of urgency. Tonight was Bridge Club for Irish Colleen, and though it was scheduled until nine, Irish Colleen capitalized on her twice-a-month adult time by drinking with her girlfriends well into the evening. Everyone knew Irish Colleen didn't actually enjoy a real friendship with any of these women, all legitimate PTA mothers who had entered their marriages with their own money and pedigree. They all knew Irish Colleen had simply come about the best luck ever catching August Deschanel. She didn't *really* belong. But none of them were stupid enough to piss off the woman who had married into the most prominent family in New Orleans and was mother to the new heir.

Madeline often wondered how much her mother knew of the icy two-faced nature of these carnivorous women. Though there was no love lost in her own relationship with Irish Colleen, she nevertheless felt a fierce protectiveness when she thought of how these women viewed her mother. As if the nature of one's birth had any bearing on their character and worth. Irish Colleen, for all her shortcomings, was twice the woman that any of those biddies were, and Madeline waited for the day they would come to eat their words. Few things rankled Madeline more than those who used their power to harm or control others.

They used Irish Colleen for her name and her connections. Madeline once confronted her mother, in an albeit angry moment, about how she allowed the women to walk all over her. Irish Colleen had smiled as she dusted the table and said, "Don't feel sorry for me, daughter. Think about what it must be like for them, knowing they have to play nice to maintain what they must see as a connection necessary for their status. It's sad, really. All that work being fake, and they'll never get anything from me outside the bottle of wine I bring to Bridge Club." She set down her rag and the smile deepened. "It's not even *good* wine."

"So why do you go?"

Irish Colleen had looked at her as if the question warranted no serious answer. "I love bridge."

Her mother didn't love much, at least not anything of a frivolous nature, so this always stuck with Madeline. Irish Colleen might have thought it was sad that the other women pretended to be her friend, but Madeline thought it equally sad that her mother had to put up with it in order to do something she actually enjoyed.

But this problem was far smaller and less consequential than the ones plaguing the world, so Madeline put it behind her, as she did with any qualms troubling their household.

She continued her mission of searching for money, safe in the knowledge her mother would be gone at least another couple of hours. She was convinced Irish Colleen had socked cash away in any number of places. She was of the old-fashioned generation, the blue collar Irish Channel crowd who didn't trust the government—*any* government, as their own in Ireland had failed them in any number of ways as well—which included the banking system, and had never broken the habit of putting her money in socks and stockings. Even when August insisted their money was safe, her mind couldn't be put at ease.

The trouble was, they spent so little time at Ophélie anymore that Madeline couldn't be sure her mother had any cash on the property. Most was probably back home, untouched and waiting for the family to return. Condoleezza would know, but even hinting at it with the old maid would lead to a world of trouble.

Madeline couldn't get access to her trust for another few years at least. Twenty-one was the legal rule written into the estate. There were provisions made for college, but no Deschanel would ever have to worry about paying for their education, not when they were behind millions of dollars in donations to higher education each year. Twenty-one was so far away... might as well be a lifetime. She could hardly stomach the idea of starting her senior year and managing through another nine months, but without money, she wouldn't get far.

She'd promised Augustus, but she'd already let him down, so, in some ways, this wouldn't be so bad. She'd ripped the bandage off already. Hell, he was probably expecting it.

Madeline knew these lies were hollow, but they sustained her. Augustus had been the only tether to the world she was a part of and the one she wished to be, and if she could convince herself that tether was severed, leaving would be as easy as slipping out and never returning.

Well, as easy as slipping out if she had the cash to sustain her.

"You shouldn't be in here."

Madeline nearly ate her heart at the unexpected sound of her little sister's accusatory voice. "I'm just looking for something, Liz. Shouldn't you be in bed?"

"I know what you're looking for."

She never knew how to read the strange things Elizabeth said. Even her empath senses couldn't land on anything specific. Elizabeth was always as cool and still as an evening on the lake. "And just what is it you think I'm looking for?"

Elizabeth's small, soft hand reached out and clasped Madeline's forearm. "It isn't too late, Maddy. You can still turn back from this path."

Madeline's hand began to tremble. She ripped her arm away and stared at her sister, without words, without quite knowing how to feel.

"Have you ever tried to slow a moving train, Elizabeth?" Madeline replied. She didn't know why she was engaging, or explaining herself. Maybe the words weren't for her. "It only stops when it hits a solid wall."

Even after Elizabeth left her alone, her ominous words put a damper on Madeline's determination. Suddenly, searching through her mother's drawers felt dirty, rather than empowering. She needed to step away from the feeling before it consumed her.

On her way to her room, she picked up on the elevated voices from some of her siblings. She stopped and leaned over the railing. This was no simple spirited debate. Colleen and Augustus' stern voices competed with Maureen's wailing, and Madeline couldn't make out a single word to piece it all together.

She should stop and listen. Figure out what was happening to cause such distress all around and go offer to help. That's what family did.

But Madeline found she could only muster a vague detachment for whatever was happening downstairs, with a family she hardly knew anymore, in a home that wasn't home.

She padded down the hall and returned to her room.

Maureen could not believe this was happening. It wasn't. It was patently impossible. There was simply no way they could truly know about her and Peter, because Peter had said the secret was safe, and Peter never lied.

Colleen looked so reasonable with the folder on her lap, but Maureen knew better. Her eldest sister was a self-righteous bitch who lived for these moments, when she could cast judgment on someone while holding herself up as the pillar of goodness.

And Augustus... why, he was no better! More subtle, perhaps, but he enjoyed his moniker of "the good son," and wore it with sanctimonious pride.

They had the nerve to sit there and accuse her as if... as if they knew anything at all! Oh, how her blood boiled! She couldn't wait to find something she could use against them, something to reveal they were not nearly as perfect as they pretended to be.

"Maureen, we're trying to help," Augustus said. Hands folded, the portrait of self-control. "What happened isn't your fault. You were taken advantage of by someone you trusted."

"We're not judging you. We love you," Colleen added.

"It's not true!" Maureen screamed. Her voice echoed across the wood and creepy plaster friezes, and she wondered if it had carried up the stairs. The last thing she needed was her other sisters joining the party against her. And Irish Colleen would be home soon...

Colleen fidgeted with the folder in her lap, which she'd had yet to open. She shared a nervous glance with Augustus. Maureen tensed. What was in it? Why hadn't she opened it yet?

"Thing is, Maureen, we know it's true."

"You don't know anything at all!" Maureen's heart beat so hard she put her hand across her chest to see if it was literally bursting away from her skeleton. It wasn't, but she could certainly feel the pulsing of the rapid *thump, thump, thump* through her flushed skin.

"I don't want to upset you even more," Colleen said. Her finger pulled at the corner of the folder. "But we have to get to the bottom of this."

"We're trying to help," Augustus said again, a broken record of useless promises.

"This whole conversation is upsetting because you two don't know what the hell you're talking about!" Maureen's eyes pricked with dark spots. Her heartrate was off the charts. What was happening? She'd begun to realize their accusations were too specific to be guesses, but she couldn't guess what might happen next. She searched her mind for any way out of this, any way to convince them this wasn't true, that whoever had told them this was a liar.

Colleen finally opened the folder. She paused and exhaled before rifling through the stack. The seconds felt like minutes to Maureen, who really thought she might pass out at any moment.

Colleen found what she was looking for and held it up.

A rush of blood and adrenaline hit Maureen like a brick and the world went dark.

SHE AWOKE TO HER SIBLINGS LEANING OVER HER. Colleen had a wet rag in her hand, held off to the side, as if she didn't quite know whether to use it. Augustus fell back on the couch in relief.

What had happened? Maureen started to ask, but there was only a momentary delay before it all came back.

Colleen had shown her a picture. That night, at the dock, on the lake. Where Maureen had feared how exposed she was, despite Peter's assurances. Where she'd been right all along.

"It's not what you think," Maureen said and then burst into tears.

They knew. There was no calling anyone a liar anymore, not when they had pictures. They knew, and now they would do everything they could to tear her and Peter apart, and Maureen's heart was no longer in danger of bursting but exploding into a million little pieces.

Her life was over! Over, over, over, over...

Colleen and Augustus held her as she cried. They didn't understand her tears. They couldn't comprehend that she was crying for a future that was now extinguished under the prying eyes of some meddling spy. Some terrible person who had ruined her entire life.

"Who?" Maureen asked. Her voice wavered. She leaned back and rolled her hands over her tear-stained eyes. "Who gave you that?"

Colleen and Augustus exchanged another look. "Charles suspected something was going on with you and asked someone to confirm," Augustus said.

"He spied on me!"

"Spying isn't right," Colleen agreed carefully. Ever the diplomat. "But I'm glad he did, in this case. Maureen, this man is taking advantage of you. I know that's hard to see... it's hard to take a step back and see it how we do, but he's preying on you."

"Peter loves me!" They didn't understand. Of course they didn't! How could they? "He's going to marry me!"

"Oh, sweetie," Colleen said, and Maureen hated her in that moment.

"Where the hell is Charles, anyway? I want him to tell me how he could betray his own sister by *spying* on her!"

Augustus frowned. Colleen tried to catch his eye, but he didn't look up. "He was supposed to be back so we could all talk to you together. I'm sorry, Maureen. You do have the right to ask him questions."

Colleen checked the grandfather clock in the corner. "He was supposed to be back thirty minutes ago." Her eyes lingered there several moments longer, and her mouth twisted in thought. "He seemed like he wanted to be here. This was his idea. He's the one—"

"Where did he go? What could be more important than ruining my life?" Maureen demanded, but a sick feeling had begun to grow deep within her. She pushed it aside, further down, afraid of what it might mean.

My Sweet Maureen. I am ill with this knowledge. Is this true?

Go away, Daddy!

How I wish I could follow you when you aren't here, but I am bound to the properties of our ancestors. I failed to protect you. I failed you.

Go away, go away, go away!

"What's important now, Maureen, is we help you through this. We need a plan. Mr. Evers needs to be held accountable for what he's done. We'll be with you every step of the way, I promise." Colleen's words all ran together, a blend of unhelpfulness. "We'll do everything we can to make this as painless as possible for you. We know you've already suffered enough."

Maureen hardly heard any of it. Not her father. Not Colleen. Something had shifted in the room, and she turned to register it.

Augustus stood at the large bay window of the parlor, looking out. Waiting.

CHAPTER 10
Huck, What Have You Done?

Charles didn't get out of the car right away. He pulled it around the back of the Big House at Ophélie, to the old covered building that had once been a livery for horses, in some long ago faraway time he couldn't even comprehend.

He wanted to stay in this moment, wedged between past and present, uncommitted to either. The last hour was a blur, because he needed it to be. For it to be any clearer would send him into madness. But he could no more face the next steps ahead of him, for undoubtedly the truth was written in his face no matter how he tried to distort it into hazy obscurity.

This unclear thing, he didn't regret it. Charles could largely only live with himself because of his innate ability to forgive his tendency to act on impulse; told himself this impulse was actually just an extension of his instinct, and one must always trust their instincts.

He should have called Colin. This was often his first thought after a bad decision, but he knew it was only his way of convincing himself he'd done wrong, instead of trusting his judgment. Colin was inevitably the counterpoint to everything Charles did; the entire opposite end of the pendulum swing. If Charles wanted to jump into a river, Colin would suggest instead finding a pool, preferably one with a lifeguard on duty. If Charles suggested a night of strippers and China White, Colin would come back with an idea to grab a six pack and crash on the couch for a movie night.

Colin was ultimately the voice of his conscience, and hot on the heels of what he'd just done, Charles needed validation, not censure.

In the end, this reminder that a man who stood by his beliefs would have no trouble facing them was what got Charles out of the car and into the house.

THE SCENE IN THE PARLOR SHATTERED HIS CONFIDENCE in a single instant. Maureen huddled alone and crying in the chaise lounge. Colleen perched awkwardly behind her, poised as if ready to either hug her or slap her, or quite possibly, both.

Augustus pounced no sooner than Charles stepped through. "Where have you been?"

The daze from the car returned. Charles was again standing on the bridge two or three miles off I-10, that spot his father took him when he was very little, deep into the Maurepas swamp. Weary from having twice his body weight a moment earlier. Weary from... the rest of it, everything leading up to him driving through the weedy-heavy trail with his low-rider Trans Am, somehow more stressed about bottoming out his baby than what caused him to turn down that road to begin with. Arms ached, burned, with the shift in mass. He felt almost weightless, but that wasn't true, or quite right, because he would never again be weightless. Some things a man could not turn back from.

"What's the matter with you? Are you on drugs?" Augustus had him by the shoulders. Charles felt his body sway with the movement, but he was no longer entirely anchored to his physical form. He floated somewhere to the left.

"No," Charles managed. He didn't know where to go from here. He took a step forward, but something else pulled him into the floor, and he looked down to see Maureen pulling at his pants, face peeled back in some fresh agony. Her mouth moved, but he couldn't make out words.

Colleen approached with a horror-stricken look, and somehow this was what pulled him back a little further into himself, and the unfolding moment.

"Huck, what have you *done*?"

Ahh, so it was Colleen who asked the right question. The first one to understand it was less important *where* he'd been.

Maureen's shrill cries pierced through, and now he understood she was asking this question, too, over and over and over. *What have you done? What have you done? What have you done?*

Charles let her hang there and looked at Augustus and Colleen with hollow eyes. He turned them on his siblings when he couldn't find any words.

"Huck?" Colleen repeated. "Where have you been? What have you done?"

Huck. Huck was such a silly name, really. It started when he was little, and one of his cousins, one of Blanche's brood, maybe Luther, couldn't say Charles. Their mother told them to try Chuck instead, but all they'd managed was Huck. Everyone thought it was so funny, everyone but Charles, who knew of only one other Huck, and it was a character in a book he'd never read.

"Huck!"

Charles snapped back to the moment with the sting of Colleen's slap. He again looked at her, at Augustus, but something in his gaze melted the look from both their faces, from anger to understanding.

"Stop asking him," Augustus said, some version of the truth coming over him as the words rolled out of his mouth. "Stop, Colleen. Don't ask anymore. If we don't know, we don't have to lie."

"Are you..." Colleen gaped at her older brother with something like disgust.

"I did what I had to do," Charles finally managed. He shrugged the shrieking Maureen from his leg and stepped away from her, from them all. "I did what I had to do."

Maureen rolled her head back and keened like an animal in its final death throes. He could muster nothing more than vague disinterest in her plight. This was her fault. He had saved her life, and yet she cried, and cried, and...

Augustus knelt down and lifted Maureen into his arms. She melted like a wilted flower, burying her face in his flannel shirt. He blew his cheeks out, eyes wide, and all he had left to offer was a shake of his head. He carried Maureen up the stairs.

Charles turned to Colleen. "Don't you dare fucking judge me. Don't you dare."

"I'm not."

"No? It's your specialty."

"I won't ask anything more. Augustus is right. But I wish you had told me first."

Charles laughed, an old, hard sound. "So you could stop me from doing what needed to be done?"

Colleen laid a hand on his shoulder. "No. So I could have helped."

FALL 1970

NEW ORLEANS, LOUISIANA

CHAPTER 11
Disappearing

Maureen wished they were all dead.

All of them.

Every last member of her unsupportive, uppity, unrelentingly unfair family.

At the same time, she didn't wish this at all, for she knew even in death she couldn't escape them. Her father was proof of this, evidence that even mourning wasn't really real, only a macabre tradition that faded to something far more sinister.

And now Peter, who plagued her in the halls of school, standing at her locker, running beside her in gym. He looked over her shoulder as she pretended to focus on a test, and watched with a vacant expression as she ate her lunch alone.

"Why, Maureen?" This was all he would say, like a broken refrain that kept skipping back to the start. "Why, Maureen?"

Why? Why? Well, she had no answer for that, and Charles still denied any wrongdoing. Colleen and Augustus turned on a blank look when asked about that night, one that wouldn't have fooled a fool. It was as if in refusing to speak of it they denied all their lives changed because of Charles' impulsiveness. Why Colleen and Augustus would side with him over Maureen was part of why she hated them, and all the others. Family first, Colleen liked to say, just like their mother, when what they really meant was protecting the family name came first, even at the cost of the happiness of the members.

What was worse, they even acted as if they'd done her a favor. A favor! Peter was her only hope; her only ticket out of her misery. It hadn't mattered to her that he was imperfect. That he had already begun to lose his looks and wasn't entirely loyal. He needed to do only one thing for her, and that was get her away from her family, and she would do everything for him. Provide him with a hot meal each night, a willing and warm bed, and as many children as his heart desired.

Colleen had said going back to school would help, because Maureen was starting high school now and that meant new experiences. Maybe she might have found a sliver of relief if the rules of ghosts, as her father explained them, weren't working against her. They were tethered to places which held personal meaning for them. In her father's case, the Deschanel properties he shuttled his family back and forth to. In Peter's, Maureen imagined, it was probably his home and the middle school, but she'd forgotten he also taught at the high school for the summer students, and when he first hovered above her locker with that sad, betrayed look, she knew her mind was not far from lost forever.

Even without him hanging around her, repeating the same question over and over, charging her with the crime, how could Maureen possibly move on? Her brother had killed her lover and would never see a day of penance from this act, despite the police coming around the house to ask questions. They said it was because Maureen was a favorite student of Mr. Evers and "got help" after school several nights per week, but the air of insinuation hanging over their words suggested they suspected a truth she'd never admit.

One didn't move on from such a thing, and Maureen's only question now was how she would survive the next four years.

"I'm sure they'll find him," Charles said as he tossed an apple in the air, the last time the police came by. Maureen gaped at him long enough for Colleen to notice and kick her under the table. But how else was she supposed to react to such a cavalier dismissal of the horrible secret they all shared? Charles came and went from whatever debauchery he engaged in, without a care, as if he hadn't *murdered* a man. Maureen marveled at how little remorse he showed. She didn't think it was an act.

Even her father actively avoided the topic, though he now knew what Maureen had done. He'd been there when it all fell apart. Seen the pictures.

How is school, Sweet Maureen? He asked, daily, as if he hadn't seen his middle daughter pressed naked into the pilings in Lake Pontchartrain.

Charles. Colleen. Augustus. August. They all knew, and they all found ways to shove the truth to the side and form a new one in its place. Maureen didn't know if her inability to do this was a sign she was more human, or less, but she could no more deny her agony than deny any other truths about herself.

When unsuspecting Irish Colleen wrote a large check to help toward the efforts of finding her daughter's "most favorite teacher," Maureen fled the room in tears and threw herself into her bed in agony.

"You have to try," her oldest sister said, appearing as if she'd been tasked with keeping tabs on Maureen's behavior. "I know you're hurting, but Mom can't know, and the authorities can't know, and that means we all have to try and bury this inside, no matter how hard it is."

"Hard? For you? How is this hard for you, Colleen?" Maureen demanded. Across the room, her bedroom door closed, a not-so-subtle chastisement to keep her voice down.

"It's hard because I love you, Maureen."

Maureen rolled her eyes to the ceiling. "Gag me with your fake love. You're not worried about me, you're worried about yourself and Huck. You're probably *relieved* he took care of the problem so it went away."

Colleen shook her head so hard her hair loosened from the bun. "Maureen, that is *not* true. Not at all. I didn't know he would..."

She swallowed the words, and a strange look passed over her face. "We shouldn't talk about it. If we talk about it, it becomes real, and it might slip in the course of conversation with others."

"Should I be shocked you care more about how this looks than how I'm feeling?"

"Your brother could go to prison!" Colleen hissed.

"He should go to prison." Maureen rolled forward on the bed and focused her eyes on her sister. "I hope he does."

Colleen backed into the closed door with a heavy sigh. "You don't mean that. I know this is hard for you—"

"You don't know a fucking thing about me."

"Watch it, Maureen. This anger will hurt you and everyone around you. What happened is terrible, but it is done, and when something is done, you gather your wits and you move on."

"Oh yeah? What if I can't?"

"You think you're suffering now?" Colleen stared her down. "Wait and see how you feel when this all unravels and you have nothing left but your anger."

While the family went about their lives in New Orleans, back and forth to school, to events, to the various places they spent their time, Colleen had never felt more alone or more concerned for all of them.

Her isolation and concern seemed to pair hand in hand, and she could not address one without solving the other.

The Deschanels had not been raised to talk about their problems. Irish Colleen had impressed upon them the age-old value of "family before all else," but this was a sentiment that stopped at the point where putting family first meant dissecting the exterior forces plaguing them. Colleen didn't know if her mother's insistence on internalizing the family's woes had started with her marriage to August—whose warmth and kindness were often confusing as these traits sat mostly at the surface; digging deeper required full mining gear and brute force—but she had carried the torch for him long after his death. They presented a tight, brave visage to New Orleans, but behind closed doors, inside the dark, gothic halls of Oak Haven or Ophélie or wherever they were, they were rotting from the inside out.

Colleen, like her mother, took up the cross of her family's survival because leaving it to chance was out of the question. Unlike her mother, she understood their mental and emotional health was as important—no, more—than protecting their reputations and wealth. But trying to crack the heavy veneer blanketing her siblings, which had taken years to grow and solidify, was a task she wasn't sure she was up to.

Charles had done something horrific. Unspeakable. His laissez faire approach to life hadn't waned—if anything, he'd thrown himself into his zest for drugs and partying with renewed fervor. Irish Colleen might take this as a sign Charles was restored to himself after a "strange spell of melancholy," but Colleen knew better. She knew better, and she knew, also, that the harder Charles tried convincing himself everything was all right, the less right things were.

What would be his undoing? Maureen's hysterics? His own behavior? A roll of fate's dice? Colleen was ill with the knowledge she carried around, but the only thing worse would be seeing her brother rot in prison. His name might reduce his sentence, but he would never have a family, have a chance to make his life right. If he'd been anyone else, Colleen would have been one of the most vocal proponents of locking him up, and the guilt laced with irony ate away at her.

Whether Maureen provided the catalyst for her brother's imprisonment, or let the knowledge fester within her, her life would never be the same. Colleen told her she'd get over it, but the words were a lie. She did not need the power of premonition to know what happened to Peter Evers would follow Maureen for the rest of her life, shaping her, for better or worse.

Meanwhile, things grew worse for Elizabeth at school. She couldn't turn off her premonitions, but she equally couldn't suffer through them alone, so she continued to share them, and this continued to become problematic not only in the classroom, but also in the broader school system. A young girl with an active imagination and some dumb luck in predictions was a solvable problem. A young girl who had accurately predicted the deaths of at least three people was something else altogether. Her situation was a bomb with a timer longer than the rest of the family's problems, and so softly ignored. But it would go off, and when it did, the solution would not be as simple this time as switching schools.

And Madeline... every morning, Colleen was certain she would wake up to find her sister gone. Being an empath was no way to live. Colleen prayed no more would be born into this family, for the only ones she'd ever known lived in a constant state of unrest.

She wished she could talk to Augustus about this, or Evangeline. But Augustus had doubled down on his business plans, even more determined, in many ways, than Charles to forget. And Evangeline, the only other child not in some kind of trouble, had taken to acting out at school to get attention in the one way she knew was always guaranteed.

Colleen wondered if she should drop her course load at university. She'd signed up for twenty-one credits, which had required special approval, and they'd tried their best to talk her down. She supposed this was her own way of dealing with everything, but it meant she wasn't around as often as she needed to be.

"Where are you?" Rory asked. He looked down at her, sweat rolling down the bridge of his nose. A few drops landed on her bare chest.

"What?"

His elbows softened. He bowed his head. "Colleen, I know when you're here, with me, in the moment, and when you've gone somewhere else."

Colleen turned her head to the side and Rory rolled off her.

He mopped the sweat from his face with his shirt and then looked at her. "You can talk to me. You don't have to pretend you're all right just to please me."

"I'm not pretending, I'm..." What? She was what? Pretending denoted that she didn't care... that she didn't love Rory, and she knew she did, she always had, even if her love for him had never quite been as passionate and devoted as his was for her. No, she wasn't pretending, because to pretend she would need to be present in a way she hadn't been, not for weeks.

Disappearing. He was right the first time when he suggested she'd gone somewhere else.

"I love you, Colleen, but I don't want..." Rory swallowed. He stared at the ceiling and drew his mouth tight, a gesture she recognized as his struggle with emotion. "I don't want you to be with me because you feel like you should. I want you to be with me because you love me, too."

"I do love you," Colleen replied, and she knew this was true, even if most of her felt numb to emotions other than worry these days. "I'm sorry, Rory. I know how this sounds, but it isn't you. Truly. It's me, and... I can't turn it off. When my family is hurting, that is. And they are."

Rory turned on his side. His smile was sad, but warm and inviting. "You can tell me. Anything, Colleen. Is it what I told Charles, about Maureen?"

Colleen of course knew Charles had been tipped off by Rory, but Rory hadn't really known anything when he told Charles Maureen was up to something. He'd heard whispers, but not specifics. Colleen had no intention of telling him, just as she'd never tell another soul who hadn't been sitting in the parlor the night Huck came in after disappearing for hours.

"It's not one thing. It never is." She pressed her palm to his damp cheek. "You did the right thing, telling Huck."

"Were the rumors true?"

Colleen paused before shaking her head. This renewed her anger with Charles, that he would put her in such a place, and with Rory of all people. "Just rumors. You know how people in this town are."

Rory nodded. "That's the truth." He angled forward and

pressed a kiss to her lips. "You take on a lot for your family. That's a huge burden for one person. It's hard enough to see after ourselves."

"It's supposed to be the job of the heir, but we all know Charles will never step up in that way. He might settle down and find some stability, but he will never be a caregiver, Rory. He'll do what his ancestors did and throw money at any problems. If I could turn it off, I would, but I can't, and, well, I won't. Between that, and school, and..."

"If you want a break..."

"No. No." As she said it, she realized she did want a break, but she couldn't treat Rory as she treated herself, using logic before emotion. A break would signal to him that she didn't love him as she claimed; that he was lower on her priority list than school, even. And while this wasn't true, because life didn't work that neatly, nothing she said would help him see the logical side if she'd just broken his heart.

Rory smiled before he could stop himself. "Okay." He kissed her again. "I'm gonna go. Call me if you need anything?"

Colleen nodded, though she would never call anyone, not even Rory, about the dark secrets eating away at her heart.

"THE POLICE CAME BY AGAIN TONIGHT." EVANGELINE tapped her heavy boots into the floor of Colleen's room.

Colleen hung her jacket on a hanger and sighed. She wanted to turn, to snap that she'd been at school all day and needed a moment to relax before being bombarded.

Instead she turned and smiled patiently. "Yes, and?"

Evangeline chewed on her bottom lip. "This is the third time. You don't think they actually believe Maureen had something to do with Mr. Evers' disappearance?"

Colleen forced a laugh. "Don't be ridiculous. Maureen was getting extra help from him, and they're just looking for any information they can get."

"Yeah, but... he disappeared over summer. Maureen wasn't his student anymore."

"They're just questioning the people who spent time with him, Evie, that's all."

"But three times."

Colleen sighed, and it was at this moment she realized she'd been in character with her family since the night Huck came in, frazzled and guilty. Even her sighs, her tilts of the head, her considered glances... they were all part of this act. "They haven't found him, and so they're going back over any lead they can find. The truth is, Mr. Evers probably doesn't want to be found. Maybe he was unhappy at home and went to start another life. Who knows? But it has nothing to do with us."

"Then why do you look so stressed about it?"

Colleen dropped her purse on the chair. The anger started in her toes and worked upward, like rays of hot light running alongside her veins. It filled her before she could stop its progression. "You know what? If I look stressed, it's because I'm taking seven classes while Maureen fails out of basic freshman math. It's because Huck can't keep his nose clean for five minutes, and Madeline seems to think she has the skill or the capacity to save the world when she can't even keep her room orderly! Never mind that Elizabeth keeps predicting the deaths of her friends' family members."

Evangeline tensed in the doorway. She crossed her arms over her chest. "Why are these your problems, Leena? Huh?"

"If I don't worry about them, who will?" When Evangeline scoffed, Colleen stormed across the room, stopping just before her. "You laugh because you have someone to care about you. Because you have *me,* who would never let anything really bad actually happen to you. You laugh instead of asking me how you can help me look after the family, because you're the only other one who lacks the self-centeredness to do it. But you don't, Evangeline. You don't offer to help. You don't come in and ask if I'd like to talk, or if you can help, because you're *so busy worrying about being left out.* Grow up, Evie! Grow. Up. You're the smartest person I know, and you're more concerned that I'm not paying attention to you, right? That we're not as close as we used to be, because I've decided that putting others first is more important than letting go and having fun? Is that right?"

Evangeline's eyes filled with tears. Her lower lip trembled. "If I haven't asked, it's because I don't think you want me to anymore. It's because I don't think you want *me* anymore."

Colleen's rage faded into the space left where her dearest sister had stood moments before.

CHAPTER 12

The Protector

Killing a man hadn't disturbed Charles' sleep patterns, but his baby sister's distress had him tossing and turning all night.

He had never given much thought to why Elizabeth's plight had always stirred him, when he was rarely moved by the angst of his other sisters. Charles, for all his other faults, enjoyed being a protector, but he'd rarely played that role, least not eagerly, for Colleen, Madeline, Evangeline, and Maureen.

He considered it now, as he watched the clock flip from 3:48 to 3:49.

Colleen had never needed him, or anyone. He'd scared off some kids bullying her in kindergarten, and instead of a thanks, she drilled him with the third degree about not needing his help, and something incomprehensible about feminism. Feminism, at five—if *that* didn't sum up Colleen, nothing did. Her strong determination often served to highlight his own failings, and it wasn't lost on him that she should have been the heir.

But that was some tough shit, because God intended Charles to be the Deschanel heir, and so he was.

Madeline and Maureen had always turned their nose up at him, and when Evangeline trained those wild, intense eyes on him, it was as if she had dissected his intentions even before he'd acted.

They were his sisters, and he loved them. Even liked them sometimes. But being home was like standing in front of the biggest goddamn mirror in the world. Like the mirror the evil queen in Snow White used, except it talked a lot of trash.

Elizabeth surely judged him as well—after all, she was raised by Irish Colleen, same as the other girls—but when she saw him, her eyes lit up and the relief filling them provided Charles with a rare sense of true purpose. It was different than the thrill of a bump of coke, or landing a new, smoking hot lay. Elizabeth was the only Deschanel who looked forward to Charles coming home, and the only one who took the sting off when he did.

One thing all the Deschanel children had in common, though, was that not one of them had asked for the abilities they were born with.

Some of them handled it better than others. Augustus hid his, for the most part. Colleen and Evangeline, both healers, never struggled the way the other girls did, and even rose to the occasion when help was needed.

Madeline, with her intense empathic senses, Maureen with whatever delusions caused her to wake screaming in the night, were reminders that not everyone was happy with the lot they'd been dealt.

As for Charles, he only had a touch of telepathy, and it worked best when he wasn't anywhere near the rest of his family, or their home. He used it to his advantage when he could and dismissed it when he couldn't.

But Elizabeth's was less a nuisance, and more of a curse. And where Irish Colleen often tried to downplay what her youngest daughter's foresight was doing to her sanity and her soul, likely in hopes Elizabeth would come to believe this as well, Charles knew better. When she cried out in the night, it was he who stood at her door to show her she wasn't alone, or crawled in beside her in bed to hold her until she fell back asleep. His bedroom was the farthest from Elizabeth's, so he knew he could not be the only one hearing her nocturnal fits, but he was the only one who ever sought to comfort her.

Elizabeth is in danger of losing her mind if she can't learn to deal with these visions in a healthy way, Colleen said once. *Indulging her, validating her fears only makes them more real.*

Charles had never wanted to hit a woman as much as he did his sister in that moment, though a part of him suspected she was right. As long as Elizabeth believed her visions were terrorizing her, they would.

But there was knowing and there was doing. And oftentimes when he found her, awake and crying, her nightshirt was covered in the dampness of her own tears and fear-induced sweats. He couldn't let her suffer, especially when everyone else in the house seemed determined the suffering was for her own good.

So, he comforted her. Loved her. Protected her.

And if he had to go beat the asses of every fifth grader in Elizabeth's class to do these things, then so fucking be it.

ELIZABETH HADN'T SAID WHICH OF THE KIDS HAD harassed her, and neither did the teacher, so if he couldn't get one of them to turn rat fink and narc, then he'd punish them all.

Charles reasoned that first recess would come an hour or two after the start of school, so he stood outside the wrought iron gates at eight in the morning and waited.

A shrill bell ripped him from his reverie. He turned to see a haphazard line of ten-year-olds streaming from the double doors of the large brick façade. A brief wave of nostalgia hit Charles as he saw kids make a beeline for their favorite section of the schoolyard. Some girls staked their claim at the white outlines of the hopscotch. A group of boys and girls flung themselves at the swings and in seconds were flying high into the air. Others gathered around in a huddled circle on an empty swatch of pavement, prepared to play jacks.

To be that innocent again, thought Charles.

The sentiment didn't last long. These children were not innocent. These insolent, bullying little shits had kept Elizabeth sleepless and crying the past couple of nights.

Charles checked his pocket for the brass knuckles. Still there. He wouldn't use them, but these little assholes didn't know that.

He'd just decided to make the circuit, starting with the hooligans on the swings, when Elizabeth finally exited the building. She hung her head, hair falling around her face like a shield. Behind her trailed five or six children, stepping on her heels, slapping at her arms. He couldn't hear their taunting words from where he stood, but he didn't need to.

This definitely made it easier for Charles, who *would have* struck the fear in God of every last kid on the playground, but preferred to only harass those who deserved it. It would be better to attack where the problem existed, and here was the problem, flashing in neon lights like a Dixie Beer sign.

Charles tossed his cigarette into the cobblestone street and squeezed through the narrow opening of the fence, near the baseball diamond. He jogged across the field until he hit cement and then slowed his pace, winded. Charles the football star had, in the past few years, been replaced by Charles the hard-partying playboy, but even in front of a bunch of sniveling kids he had an image to maintain.

By the time he reached the cluster of shits antagonizing his sister, Charles was well recovered. He straightened his collar and stepped right into the middle of their bully-fest, wedging himself between the other children and his sister. Elizabeth, at first surprised and then, eyes filled with complete awe, pressed her small body into his side and burst into tears.

"Huck," she whispered, and that seemed to be all she could say.

"I take it you little pisswads are the ones fucking with my sister?" He beamed a smile at them. His teeth gleamed, and he hoped he looked less like the handsome heir the world saw him as and more like the monster emerging from their closets and under their beds.

The children sputtered their responses. None put together words anywhere near resembling a sentence.

And then one brave boy managed, "She's our friend. We're just playing."

Charles ran his hands over his baby sister's matted hair. "Playing? Swell, let's play a game where I make all of you cry, too. Yeah? Sound like fun? Sounds like so much fucking fun, right?"

One little girl, with long black hair tied in the ugliest bow Charles had ever seen, burst into tears.

"No?" Charles laughed. "Well, it sounds like fun for me. Because if you can dish it out, you can handle it, you spoiled, ungrateful little assholes." He smiled at the little girl crying. "Not so much fun when you're on the other end of it, now is it? Not so much fun when you're not king of the fucking jungle anymore?" He moved his hands around the small group, noting a larger group had gathered to watch. "Are we having fun yet?"

"She... she... said my uncle was going to die," a little boy stammered. "She started it!"

Charles sighed and leaned in. "I don't know how to tell you this, son, but if Elizabeth says your uncle is going to die... well, the old man's a goner."

The boy erupted in tears. Elizabeth whimpered at Charles, clutching her hands around his waist.

"So, look. Here's how it's gonna be, you spawns of Satan." Charles squeezed his sister. "If I hear of any of you touching my sister... no, so much as *looking* at her sideways, I'm coming after you. You might be thinking, he can't do anything to us, we're kids!" He nodded, smiling, leveling his toothy grin on every single child individually. "True. But I can hunt down *every single one of your fathers* and beat their asses into oblivion. I can have them blacklisted from every financial establishment and country club in New Orleans, and you'll all be eating Cracker Jacks out of toilet bowls, ya dig? And there isn't a judge in town I can't buy or persuade to let me walk for doing it." He cackled. "And you know it, don't you? You know who Elizabeth is, so you know who I am. And you know that when you're visiting your daddies in Touro Infirmary, after I put them there… on your bus pass, since that's all you'll be able to afford when I'm done with your families… I'll be drinking cognac and partying my way up and down Uptown, free as a bird."

There must be a darker side to himself, something far past troublemaking and veering into the territory of outright wickedness of the soul, for Charles drew great pleasure from the fear in the children's faces, fear he'd created. The urge to say more, to say far worse, crept to the tip of his tongue, and oh how wonderful it would be to see them dissolve into a puddle of their own tears! These hateful, terrible shits who hadn't been raised to play nicely with others; whose parents were likely bullies, too.

But the face of his father appeared before Charles, and he stilled the venom bubbling up within him. Any signs of mischief had faded from the eyes of these children, replaced by the kind of deep terror that reduces even adults to helpless infants. The other kids, those looking on, shared that fear, and he knew that, by the time the bell rang again, all the children of the school would know the price of messing with Elizabeth Deschanel.

Charles knelt and kissed Elizabeth on the forehead. "And you'll tell Huck exactly which of these little assholes don't abide by the rules, won't you?"

Elizabeth nodded, playing along, though they both knew she would never share names, for his words were true. He would go after their fathers and would never see consequence for it. And, just like with that Evers douchebag, he wouldn't lose a minute of sleep.

"So, we square?"

Charles didn't wait for an answer. He pulled Elizabeth along and walked away from the crowd of whimpering children, and lit a cigarette.

. . .

THAT NIGHT, CHARLES LAY AWAKE, HIS BABY SISTER'S hair spread across his chest. Her light snores lulled him slowly into restful sleep. He had no doubt what he'd done was right and was good. He would do anything to right a wrong done against his family.

Anything.

This was why he was heir.

CHARLES AWOKE TO HIS MOTHER'S SCREECHING FROM the doorway. It wasn't the first time he'd risen to this sound, and it would not be the last, but this particular decibel of shrillness set his alarm bells tingling.

Elizabeth had returned to her own bed sometime during the night, but he'd left his arm looped back over the pillow and now it ached from the lack of movement. He squinted against the light spilling in from the hallway and propped himself half-up with his good arm.

"What time is it?"

Irish Colleen stormed into the room. She towered over him, despite her small stature. "It's time for you to pull your life together, Charles. It's time for you to understand consequences so maybe, *maybe,* you'll understand you cannot do as you please, whenever you please. This time, you've ruined someone else's life."

"Ma, I have no clue what you're running on about." Charles shielded his eyes and groaned.

"Running on? You and your mouth, Huck. I swear on the Holy Cross, not even St. Jude the Apostle would take on this lost cause," Irish Colleen hissed. "I have always said, I don't care who you run around with, but use protection! Is that so hard?"

"Ma, please, just tell me what I did already, so we can get this over with."

Irish Colleen threw a folded piece of paper at the end of the bed. Charles massaged his dead arm as he watched his mother with growing caution. He narrowed his eyes and reached for the letter.

She snatched it from his hands before he could read it. "It will take you too long to read it. You got a young girl pregnant, and I do mean *girl*. She's a freshman in high school." Irish Colleen's mouth turned into a disgusted sneer. "Pregnant. I should have known this would happen eventually! What luck, that this floozy is the first. You are not the man your father was. August is rolling in his grave, and I hope to heaven he doesn't blame me for any of this."

Charles didn't hear the rest of what she said. Pregnant. A girl was pregnant, and he was the father, and... how? He'd always used protection.

Eh, not always. Not when he was too high or drunk to remember. Not if pulling out a rubber dampened the mood.

"Who is she?" he asked, and then braced himself for his mother's venom.

"Her name is Shelly, but I suspect that doesn't help you narrow it down, now, does it?"

It didn't help, except that he was able to exclude most of the girls he and Dan Weatherly ran with, as there were no Shellys in the trust fund crowd, not that he'd met. But it didn't exclude Dan's wider net of girls not quite as privileged, but certainly eager. His parties were filled with girls like this.

"Must have been someone you trifled with this spring, because she's several months along, according to her mother." Irish Colleen closed her eyes. "They didn't ask for money, but I'll have the Sullivans send enough to take care of this mess and then some."

"I thought abortion was a grievous sin?" Charles couldn't resist. He was no angel, but then, neither was his mother, despite what she liked to portray.

"You're not too old for me to whip you."

"Or slap me," Charles quipped.

"I won't have some illegitimate bastard coming after your inheritance, Huck. Whether you care, or understand, or care to understand, your father, God rest his soul, left me in charge of your future. Unless you plan to *marry* this girl you can't even remember, then this cannot happen. And I will answer to God for this sin, yes, but I'll be damned if I don't do what my husband asked me to do, as his soul slipped on to heaven." Irish Colleen crossed herself and looked up. "Your transgressions are my cross to bear, for my sins."

Charles rolled his eyes, but inside, his chest tightened. His stomach fluttered. While she rambled on about his sins, he'd searched for the answer, as to who this girl might be. He narrowed it down to the eclipse party. Spring. Freshman. Shelly. He couldn't remember her name, but he would never forget the, *I'm fourteen, daddy.* Even Charles had *some* scruples, and he'd felt sick about his tryst with a girl no older than Maureen. But then he'd forgotten about it, shelved it next to the rest of his sins, until now.

"Shelly," he said, for the first time aloud, something he hadn't known when he'd let her ride him through the weirdness of the eclipse, drug-sick and far from himself.

"Yes, Shelly, not that it matters," Irish Colleen snapped. "Whatever her name is, she isn't going to bear your child, Charles August Deschanel. No woman who is not your wife will ever bear your child. I won't allow it." She stood, folding the letter. She placed it neatly into the fold of her apron. "What's more, it's time, I can see now, to move forward with what I've been putting off too long."

Charles closed his eyes and looked away. He was numb.

"It's time to start planning a marriage for you."

Irish Colleen closed the door, and the room was again swathed in darkness.

CHAPTER 13

White Rabbit

Twenty-seven was too young to die.

This was Madeline's last coherent, lucid thought before the acid really took its hold. There was always that waiting period, sometimes ten, twenty, or even thirty minutes, after the hit had dissolved on the tongue, but nothing had shifted in the outside reality. Each time, though she knew it took time to stretch through the system and into the brain, she wondered if it was a bad dose, if she'd be stuck in sober reality while her friends floated through the world, tripping daisies, oblivious to all but the moment.

Jill and Josh didn't wait for the LSD to make its mark. They were squirreling around on the floor before the hits even dissolved, and Madeline didn't know if they wanted her to watch or just didn't care if she did.

"Get a room," she said as her eyes rolled.

"This is our room, sister," Jill mumbled between sloppy kisses and the crinkling sound of Josh fumbling with the condom wrapper, and Madeline realized with a sinking dread that if she stayed, she *would* be trapped in the back of this tiny, smelly van with the sound and smell of their sex.

The dread deepened when she understood she'd have to go

home and ride out her trip there. If she couldn't manage to hide in her room for the next twelve hours...

Slurp. Suck. Moan.

Madeline stifled her disgust at the quickly escalating situation and reached for the old rusted van door. With a grunt and a heave, she flung it open. It made a pained squeal as it moved along the rutted track. For a moment she forgot where she was. An empty parking lot yawned ahead, and the only other inhabitants were some abandoned shopping carts and the garbage not yet picked up.

She hopped out onto the cement. Her effort to close the ancient door behind her was only half-hearted, and it reopened again, but the lovers inside didn't notice.

The Schwegmann's off Tchoupitoulas. Not that close to Oak Haven, but not exactly Timbuktu, either. Far enough that walking would take too long, but she had no money for a taxi. That left only one option.

Her thigh still ached from the assault borne by the needles at the tattoo parlor earlier. She'd always wanted the butterfly etched into her flesh, the wings that would carry her away. Now that she had it, she was distraught to discover she felt no more capable of flying.

Madeline slung her beaded bag across one shoulder and stuck her thumb into the night.

EVANGELINE WAS HALFWAY THROUGH HER PSYCHOLOGY studies, serving out the remainder of her nightly homework sentence with eyes glazed and utterly unfocused, when Madeline came stumbling through the front door of Oak Haven like a bull in a china shop.

Had her entrance been less dramatic, Evangeline might have had time to warn her. *Mama is on a warpath, and the target is you, sis.*

Irish Colleen launched into sentry mode in the foyer before Madeline could settle on a place to drop her ugly bag. Madeline was too busy spinning—for reasons Evangeline couldn't begin to comprehend, though she suspected heavy drugs, because it was always drugs with Maddy—to notice, but Irish Colleen's heavy disappointment boomed through the house with such force that Evangeline inadvertently let her notebook slip off her lap and land on the floor. It remained there, forgotten, as she waited to see how this particular family episode would unfold.

"What are you on?" cried Irish Colleen, sniffing about her daughter as if LSD had a scent. She snapped her fingers before Madeline's eyes, further demonstrating the lack of depth in her knowledge of how drugs worked. Madeline erupted into what Colleen liked to call, "pothead giggles," though they were now mostly everyday giggles for Maddy.

"What am I on? What am I off?" Madeline parroted between her uncontrolled and inexplicable laughter. Her face was a sheen of sweat and runny makeup, and Evangeline wished she could hit pause long enough to go in and wipe her down. It wasn't helping the already unhinged situation.

Irish Colleen ran a finger down her daughter's sweaty face and regarded the results in pure disgust, as if sweat alone could mortally offend. "Answer me, Madeline, or so help me God, I will call in every last one of your father's relatives to pull the answer right out of your head."

"I'm *remembering* Jimi and Janis tonight," Madeline said, which she clearly expected to explain away everything.

"Jimi and Janis? Are these some of your junkie friends? You'll forgive me if I can't remember them all, their personalities blend together."

"Jimi *Hendrix* and Janis *Joplin*," Madeline slurred. She giggled at something in the corner and ran her hands across the air in front of her.

"And they are?"

"Incredible musicians! They're now gone... gone, and I'm so sad. So, so sad." But Madeline's face was an ear-to-ear smile, and Irish Colleen slapped it away.

"Oh, yes, *now* I know who you're talking about. I read the paper!" Irish Colleen's hands were a fixture on her hips now. "Both of them died of some kind of drug overdose. The same path *you're* heading down if you don't pull your life together, Madeline!"

Madeline's smile failed, replaced by the comically serious look of someone trying especially hard to appear sober. "You know nothing about my life, Mama. Nothing."

Irish Colleen reached into her apron. In her fist was a crinkled sheet of paper. "I know you're already failing all but one of your classes and if you don't fix this in the next couple weeks, you've already killed your chance of graduating at the end of your senior year!"

Madeline frowned in a confused way. She lost her footing, stumbling back. When she reached for the paper, Irish Colleen yanked it away and out of reach.

"Why do I even bother when you're like this? Why? God only knows! Your father in heaven knows, but he couldn't be troubled to stay with us and see you through your difficult years. The Good Lord knows I've tried." She looked up. "I never asked for this."

"No? I guess that's what happens when you marry a desperate widower and shoot out babies like a spring rabbit!" Madeline exclaimed. She grasped the bannister for support, but she seemed clear for the first moment since her arrival. "Failure doesn't get whisked away because you insist to God you never asked for the job in the first place."

Irish Colleen balked. "Are you saying I've failed as your mother?"

"You say it, Mama, every day. Every day. Except you say it like *I'm* the failure. You've done everything you could, right? Everything except try and understand *who I am and why I am this way!*" Madeline's footsteps rang against the hardwood flooring, and Evangeline crept to the doorway for a better view. "You never asked for defective children, huh? But we did? We asked for it? I asked to feel every drop of pain and sadness for everyone around me? Augustus asked to be used, over and over, to get us what we want? Lizzy asked to see everyone's fate? Maureen asked to talk to the dead?"

"Maureen does not talk to the dead!"

Madeline threw back her head and laughed. "Okay, Mama. You're right. You know all of us so well."

Irish Colleen turned away and snorted. "Why am I arguing with you? You won't even remember this conversation. You never do. Nothing ever changes."

"You never change, so why would anything else?" Madeline's joy had faded entirely. Her eyes clouded with tears.

Irish Colleen stormed from the room without another word. Madeline choked back a sob in her throat. She reached for her messy, sweaty hair and pulled it into a tight knot at the back of her neck, and then released it, rolling forward, hands to her knees, with a gasp.

Evangeline didn't understand her sister. She never had. Madeline's heart was big, but her priorities were out of whack, and she refused to listen to reason. In this, she agreed with her mother.

But she couldn't be aligned with Irish Colleen in this moment. Her mother was the one in the wrong now, the immovable force pushing her daughter further from the love and support that might eventually lead her down the right path. Irish Colleen, in her own stubbornness, was too blind to see how her righteous anger enabled Madeline's descent into madness.

Madeline was alone. Even Augustus had a falling out with her, though Evangeline knew nothing of the details.

"She doesn't understand you," Evangeline said. She held her breath at the announcement of herself, for she knew it wasn't right to eavesdrop.

"No shit," Madeline murmured, sniffling. "I can't stay here, Evie. I'm sorry. You understand, right? I've tried, but no one, *no one*, knows how to hurt me like she does, and I'll die if I don't get out soon."

Evangeline nodded, not because she understood exactly, but because she suspected Madeline wasn't wrong about her future if she didn't make some kind of change. "I know, Maddy, but please don't leave. Where would you even go? You don't have any money, or any…" She almost said friends, but that seemed a cruel point to stick on the end.

"Does it matter? Is it so much better here that a little uncertainty is so scary?"

Evangeline shrugged. "I don't know."

"You could come with me, you know."

"Me?"

"Why not?" Madeline snatched her bag from the chair. It grazed the floor as it dangled. "Really, why not? No one even pays attention to you, Evie. You're the most normal of all of us, the absolute smartest and most talented, and where that should count for something, it counts for exactly nothing in the Deschanel household. Whoever is most fucked up at the moment has *always* gotten all the love, or all the hate in this house, and if you think that'll change when I'm gone, well, I have some oceanfront property in Arizona to sell you."

Evangeline tensed at the brutal honesty. Of course she knew all this. It wasn't exactly breaking news. But it still hurt to hear it aloud. "You'd really want me to come with you and slow you down?"

Madeline threw her arms out. Her bag shimmered as it came up, the handles still wrapped around her hands. "I've got nothing *but* time, Ev. I don't care about school. I never did. I only stayed for Aggie, and now…" She rubbed her hand over her nose. "And now, nothing. There's nothing for me here. So you wanna come? Find some real meaning in this world, with someone who won't treat you like you're a freak of nature?"

Evangeline pursed her lips. Thinking. "Did you really get high because of Janis Joplin and Jimi Hendrix?"

"I get high because it's the only time my mind is free of the pain," Madeline replied without missing a beat. "It's the only way I know to block out all the feelings and experiences of the world. To blunt them. I know you all think I'm a crisis junkie, but I've just learned how to live with who I am. And that answer is, I either help solve the world's problems, or I lose myself. According to Mama, both make me a failure. So you tell me, Evangeline, where is the win in any of this?"

An acute sadness stole over Evangeline, and she wanted to hug her sister, hug her tight and squeeze their sadness until it spilled over, but she didn't. "Colleen is too busy for me lately. I'm alone, too."

"Who said I was alone?"

Evangeline said nothing.

Madeline sniffled. "Yeah, okay, you dope, I guess I am. I guess I am alone, and if you wanna come with me, I 'spose that solves two problems, yeah?"

Evangeline nodded. She swallowed a hard breath and then nodded again. "Okay. I need to pack a bag. I have stuff that's important to me that I can't leave here."

"Sure. Pack one me for one, too, will ya?" Madeline smiled through her tears, and Evangeline had never realized until then how beautiful her strange older sister was.

"Yeah, okay. You'll pick me up?"

"No, darlin'. I can't come back here. Meet me at the train station tonight around nine. There's a train to D.C. leaving around ten, and if you can manage to filch some cash, we can be on it."

Evangeline supposed this was always what Madeline meant by leaving, but it still opened a pit in her stomach to think of leaving the only town she'd ever known, for one that, at least according to the news channels her mother watched, was rife with crime and protests and other dangers completely foreign to her. She'd committed to it without really giving it much thought at all.

"Nine," she repeated, already wishing she'd just kissed her sister goodbye and left it at that.

"Nine. Be there or be square," Madeline said, and then she was gone.

No matter how many times Maureen blinked her eyes, the dark spots didn't go away. The tingling in her hands, which was now also in her feet, only intensified as her heartbeat pulsed into her vision, her breaths. The police officer sitting across from her wore the appropriate level of concern and gentle handling for someone of her age, but he didn't know what she knew. What she had *done.*

The body of Peter Evers had been found, and now, and now...

"I'm sorry, Maureen, would you like me to repeat the question?"

She struggled to swallow through her dry mouth. Colleen squeezed her hand in encouragement, but this didn't help, not at all. Colleen was just like Charles. She wasn't her friend, or even her sister, not right now.

"Yes, sir. Please."

Officer Beauregard smiled patiently. He looked at Colleen. "Are you sure we shouldn't wait for your mother to return?"

Colleen shook her head. "No, Officer, it's fine. She won't be back until she's finished her errands, which could be quite late depending on traffic."

That was a lie, at least in how confident the words rolled off Colleen's tongue. No one knew when Irish Colleen would be back, because she and Charles were off looking for Madeline, a peculiar and emotionally charged situation Maureen hadn't even begun to think about. Not with her heartbeat shoving her shirt out from her skin in violent thrusts, a phenomenon *surely* this nice police officer could see.

"Very well." He flipped the page in his small, tattered notepad. With another smile to Maureen, he said, "Can you tell me again when you last saw Mr. Evers for help with your studies?"

Maureen squinted, hoping this was a convincing show in how little regard she gave such a memory. Her tongue was molten lava, burning the back of her teeth. "It would be right before school let out, sir."

"You don't remember exactly when?"

"No, sir."

"Perhaps if you think about the final events of your eighth

grade, that might help with the recollection. For example, did you stop going to see him before or after your final tests?"

Colleen's hand came down over hers in a subtle command. She'd been picking at the skin around her nails so hard she'd started to bleed. Maureen shoved them under her fidgeting legs. "Um... before?"

"Are you certain, or is that a guess?"

"Officer, Maureen is barely fourteen. She doesn't keep a calendar, or a planner, or we could check that for you. She was getting help from other teachers as well, not only Mr. Evers."

The officer, though, ignored Colleen and awaited Maureen's reply.

"A guess," Maureen said.

"Would there have been any need for you to get help from Mr. Evers after your final tests?"

"No, sir, I suppose not, with all schoolwork being done and grades posted."

"Then your last session with Mr. Evers would have been before finals? Is that correct?"

"Yes, sir, now that you say it that way, I'm quite sure I never saw him after finals. There was no need."

Colleen tensed.

Officer Beauregard scribbled notes. His mouth twisted in thought as he tapped the pencil eraser against the paper. When he looked up, his smile had dissolved. "Several of your classmates have said they saw you with Mr. Evers after finals."

Maureen's face exploded with heat. "Oh? I suppose... I mean, maybe, yes, I probably also saw him after finals just like I saw all my other teachers after finals, to say goodbye."

"Do you typically see your teachers outside of school?"

"Well, no, I mean, unless we run into them at Schwegmann's or something." Maureen's hands turned to fists under her legs and she was absolutely positive the sweat rolling down her forehead was about to drop into her eyes.

Officer Beauregard nodded. "Of course, but I'm not talking

about incidental run-ins. I'm asking if you ever had occasion to see your teachers outside of school intentionally. Say, for dinner, or just to hang out."

Colleen chimed in. "Our mother is known to host dinner parties, Officer. It's possible we've had many of our teachers over at the house. Perhaps even Mr. Evers."

"I'm not talking about here at your home, Miss Deschanel," he replied without taking his eyes off Maureen. He flipped back a few pages in his notes and said, "Specifically, some of your classmates noted they've seen you in his car with him. Just the two of you."

If Maureen didn't throw up it would be a Christmas miracle. "I... uh..."

"He'd given you a ride home a few times, isn't that right, Maureen?" Colleen urged.

"Yes," Maureen said quickly. "A few times."

The officer checked his notes again. "One of them said you were seen together merging onto I-10 from Mid-City, and another down by the old Daigle's fish treatment plant, on the river. Those are both in the complete opposite direction of the school or home, so there must have been another reason you were with Mr. Evers in his car."

"That's ridiculous," Colleen said with a laugh. "How would people even be in the right place to make such sightings? This sounds like a lot of nonsense."

The officer didn't seem to find this as humorous. "Those are just two of five occurrences of the two of you being sighted together, and the others are questionable locales as well. Now, Maureen, I'm sure there's a very reasonable explanation for these, and if you'll explain it to me, that will help me a good lot."

Colleen jumped to her feet. Maureen felt the heat radiating from her sister. "Can we take a quick break? I need to use the ladies' room."

Officer Beauregard folded his hands over his notebook and sat back, with a mild look of disappointment. "Of course."

Five minutes passed. The officer hardly looked at Maureen, which was a small blessing, but his scrutiny of his notes during this period didn't put her at ease. People had seen her with Peter. Seen them in places there was no reasonable explanation for. And this officer, he was a smart guy. He knew more than he'd revealed, and there was no telling what else he'd held back on. This was his third visit to the house, and even Maureen understood that was not just simple protocol.

When Colleen returned, she was not alone. Augustus shuffled in behind her, and Maureen went rigid as she processed what his presence meant.

Augustus introduced himself to the officer, who remarked how much Augustus resembled his father. Augustus moved subtly into a fighter's stance, one leg in front of the other, and his fingers twitched.

"We appreciate you coming to see us and questioning Maureen. It's safe to say, you're satisfied now and won't be needing anything more from Maureen." He reached forward and pulled the notebook from the officer's hands. After a quick scan, he tore out a few pages and handed it back. "In fact, I'm sure you weren't even here today."

"No, sir. I sure wasn't," Officer Beauregard replied. He rose and thanked Augustus for his time, then left without another word.

"Hell's bells," Maureen whispered.

Augustus stared stone-faced until he heard the officer's car fire up. Then he turned to Colleen and said, "Never again. If this is how you all see my contribution to the family, fixing every problem by wiping away all semblance of consequence, then count me out."

"I know, Aggie, I wouldn't have asked if I thought there was any other way."

"There's always another way, Colleen."

"I won't ask again."

Augustus laughed. "Oh. You will." He shook his head and left them standing there.

NINE CAME AND WENT. TEN PASSED AS WELL, AND BY eleven, Madeline stopped checking her watch.

It was possible Evangeline was caught. Irish Colleen, Charles, Augustus, they were all bullies of a different flavor, and Colleen could ignore Evangeline and still hold sway over her. Her spell was that strong.

She hadn't really expected Evangeline to show up, anyway. Why would she? She had no strong reason to stay, but she also had no reason to leave. She was ignored for the most part, but that also meant she wasn't living in constant turmoil. If Madeline were Evangeline, she probably wouldn't leave, either. She was passionate enough to decry comfort, but practical enough to appreciate it.

Outside, the rain picked up. The weather often served to punctuate her choices, and the symbolism was never lost on Madeline. But after the storm was always the blossom of new life, and new experiences. She'd given up her creature comforts, but once she got on her feet, things would be okay.

With a sad look back at the station, she shoved her hands in her pockets and trudged down the flooded sidewalk, destination unknown.

CHAPTER 14

One Less Witch

No one in Oak Haven had slept well since Madeline ran off.

The worry shifted from sibling to sibling. Irish Colleen spun herself into a frenzy for days, calling every hospital, forcing a vow from the Chief of Police to keep an eye out for Madeline, and then switched to a subdued daze where worry lived on the outside of the bubble pushing her forward. Charles declared Madeline a drama queen on day one, but by the second day was pounding the pavement night and day in search of her. Colleen found him huddled by the hearth one night, shaking, and she pieced together that he'd been too busy to satiate his cocaine fix and was jonesing from the oversight.

Maureen and Evangeline joined the search, but Irish Colleen put a swift end to their involvement when it occurred to her the impact this might have on their schooling. Elizabeth stressed quietly in her room, but kept her own counsel. Everyone wanted to ask her what she might know, but no one dared. She could help keep hope alive, yes, but she could also destroy it forever.

That left Augustus, who at first pretended he wasn't invested in the situation, but the façade crumbled fast when Madeline didn't return. She'd always returned, and now she'd seemingly fallen off the map of the world. Whatever residual anger lived in him, for reasons he'd never explained to any of them, and Colleen suspected never would, he shrugged it off now.

One night, Augustus was out looking for Madeline and Evangeline had snuck off to be with him. Irish Colleen, who despite the Irish in her rarely found herself too far in the cups, nursed a tumbler of whiskey. An old photo of August out at the lake sat in her lap. She caressed it, pausing here and there to wipe her tears.

"Mama?"

"Do you know I was raised in a single bedroom shotgun cottage with seven siblings? Our mother gave us the bedroom, though it wasn't much of anything. She slept on the couch when she wasn't working one of three jobs."

Colleen had heard this story so many times she could finish her mother's sentences, but said nothing.

"There was nothing she wouldn't give for her children, even when she had nothing to give." She finished off her amber drink. Her unsteady hand reached for the bottle without looking up, and Colleen took the opportunity to slide it out of her reach.

"Maddy dared say I married your father for the wrong reasons," she continued. Her words had a slurred edge, but she wasn't so drunk Colleen would have to devise a way to get her up to her bed safely. "She had no idea how I loved Eliza!"

The name of August's first wife was rarely spoken in the house. August met her in college up north and married her for love, in a time when Deschanels were still arranging marriages for their advantage. He loved her through her barrenness, despite the pressure to have an heir, and he loved her until she breathed her last after a nasty dance with cancer. And just as no one mentioned Eliza, no one dared suggest that the marriage between August and Irish Colleen, barely a month after Eliza was cold in the grave, was anything less than love as well.

But everyone knew better just the same.

August married once for love and his heart got broken. When he married again, it was duty driving him. He didn't have the heart to go find love again, and so he looked at what was right in front of him. And August, a man who had first followed his heart, became a man who understood his duty, and in his middle age became the father of seven children by a woman who had nursed the only woman he'd ever loved.

"People say a lot of things when they're hurting, Mama," Colleen offered, stopping short of taking a side. While she fancied herself a maternal figure in the household, they all knew Irish Colleen was harder on Madeline than any of them. Madeline had been August's darling. Of all of them, she was the one he chose to nurture, perhaps believing she had it the hardest as the one absorbing the pain of others. Or maybe because she looked just like him. Whatever his reasons, Madeline was punished for this special attention now.

"Was your father in love with me?" She tossed back a liquid-less sip with a frown and then set the glass aside altogether. "Only God can say. He loved me in the language I was raised in, and that was all I could have ever asked of him. He provided."

"We'll find her," Colleen said. Where was Charles? He was better at this, when their mother was in the type of mood where whimsy trumped her usual pragmatism. "Augustus will find her, and if he can't, Aunt Ophelia will know what to do. She knows the abilities of every last one of us, and surely there's someone in the family who can find her."

"Ophelia? That old coot?" Irish Colleen belted out a grating laugh. "I tolerate her because it's what August would want. If that woman wasn't a Deschanel, she'd be begging for change outside Tulane Stadium."

A wave of anger swept over Colleen, but she channeled it to her hands, which she curled into balls. "That's not true. You don't mean that, either. You're upset about Maddy."

"Upset?" Irish Colleen rolled her head back against the plush couch pillow. "Oh my dear, she's doing us all a favor! One less mouth to feed! One less bloody *witch* to worry about!"

Colleen left her mother in a sputtering, drunken fit of tears and laughter.

RORY'S HEARTBEAT WAS THE ONLY SOUND IN THE DARK bedroom. She rode the rise and fall of his chest as he surrendered to his dreamless sleep. She sensed nothing in him, no turmoil, no strain or stress to interrupt his rest. Certainly no mother like hers, armed with words aimed right for the heart.

Sleep wasn't in the cards for Colleen that night. This wasn't an especial departure from most nights, where she subsisted on less than five or six hours sustainably, but her family's angst had begun to catch up to her, like compound interest. Not one of them was in a good place, and Colleen felt the sting of that like a personal failure.

Colleen carefully slipped out of Rory's embrace, settling his bare arm across his chest. She sneaked from the room on tiptoes and closed the door with a light click.

At this late hour, there'd be no one else in the bathroom she shared with her sisters, but she locked it behind her anyway. Normally the lack of personal boundaries wasn't a big deal, but tonight she needed to be alone. Not to be in her own head, but to be out of it. To clear it.

Tomorrow, she'd go see Aunt Ophelia. No matter what Irish Colleen thought of her, Colleen knew her to be the wisest woman in this family. Hell, the wisest woman she'd ever met. As the scalding hot water passed over Colleen's skin, turning her flesh an angry red, she knew this was the answer. Asking for help wasn't a failure, not when the alternative was worse.

Ophelia would know.

She would know what to do about Madeline. About Charles. About Maureen. About Elizabeth. About Augustus. Even Evangeline, who'd flown under the radar lately, but surely must be struggling, too. Of all of them, Colleen wore her sister Evangeline's aloofness as a deeply personal failure, knowing full well that if her other siblings didn't need her so much, she and Evangeline would still be as close as ever.

Colleen lowered herself to the small seat in the corner of the shower. She pressed her face against the porcelain tile and closed her eyes, clearing her mind entirely, as Aunt Ophelia had taught her.

THE EXERCISE IN RELAXATION WORKED. WHEN COLLEEN returned to the room, her eyelids were drooping and a lazy softness had passed over her. Yes, she could sleep now, even if only for a few hours.

When she slipped into the room, soft noises gave her pause. Kissing sounds and... moaning. A thin swath of moonlight crossed the room, but it wasn't enough to cut through the dark and reveal the source of the shapes moving in the corner.

Colleen flipped the light switch. She stumbled back into the wall. There was no way she was seeing what she was seeing, and yet...

Evangeline straddled Rory. She was bent forward over him, her wild hair sprayed out over her naked back, like so many corkscrews.

Rory made a series of confused sounds, flailing about the bed. He looked up at Evangeline and tossed her to the side, gaping in horror as he did, scrambling back against the headboard and to the edge of the bed.

"What the..." His hands were an erratic mess as they traveled over his skin for answers. "I didn't know... how the hell..."

Colleen fought to keep her knees from buckling. She understood without Rory needing to explain, though she didn't stop him from his desperate attempts to try. She knew what a heavy sleeper he was. What Evangeline had done.

Evangeline pulled her nightshirt against her skin. Her face was damp with tears. "I tried to tell you... I tried to tell you, Colleen, that I *needed* you."

"Get out of my room."

"You wouldn't listen. I didn't know how to get your attention, and then Maddy wanted me to go with her, and I almost did, but then I tried... again to tell you, and you had more important things than me. You always do now."

Colleen's eyes trembled in their sockets. Her breaths came short and shallow, and it was a miracle, she thought, that they were coming at all, really. She couldn't look at either of them, not even Rory who was just the witless dupe.

"And I was wrong, but now I need you out of my room, Evangeline. I need you out of my room before I cross this carpet and strangle the life from your body."

Evangeline fought the tangle of blankets as she stumbled from the bed. Hysterical sobs racked her body. "I only kissed him. I knew he'd think it was you. I only kissed him, Colleen."

Colleen looked at her, then, finally, with ice in her heart. "Bully for you, because you just destroyed our relationship with only a kiss."

"*Please*, Colleen!"

"Out of here, now!"

Evangeline fled the room in tears, dropping her nightgown as she did. When she reached down to grab it, Colleen slammed the door in her face.

She was alone with Rory.

"Colleen, I swear to you—"

"No need," she replied. "I know what happened."

His whole body wilted with heavy relief. "Oh thank God. Jesus. Why did she do that?'

"I need you to go, Rory."

"What? Leena, that wasn't—"

"I'm not mad at you." Colleen needed to sit, and soon, or her body would do it for her. All the blood had drained from her extremities. The stars in her eyes would come next. "But I need you to leave."

He came to her and wrapped her in his warms. She wiggled out. "Colleen, I don't understand."

"I just can't do this right now."

"What?"

"This. Us."

Rory's hands fell back to his sides. Colleen couldn't look at him. Couldn't see in his eyes what she felt in his deflated energy. "Us?"

"I love you," she said, the first time she'd spoken the words first, and not out of duty to respond. "But I'm flailing, Rory. Flailing and failing. Evangeline is right. I wasn't there, and I didn't listen. And she's not the only one. I've done it to all of them."

"That's not fair to you." He crossed his arms over his chest, and in that moment, they were friends again, the second boundary closed. "I have never known anyone who does more for their siblings than you. No one. My brother Colin is a good guy, but do you think he loses sleep over me? Or Patrick, or Chelsea? There's love and then there's you. You can't take it all, Colleen. We aren't built for it."

"Maybe most aren't," she agreed. "Maybe even me. But asking me not to try is asking me not to be who I am. This is who I am, Rory. And not just today. I don't need anyone to divine my future to know I'll be leading this family one day. Not because I should, but because I'll pick up the torch no one wants to carry."

"That's not fair."

"Life isn't fair."

"I really do love you, Colleen. The real kind."

She lowered her head and chanced a smile. "I know. And if I were anyone else, that would be enough."

"But you're not anyone else," he said slowly. He reached for his shirt. Then his pants. "I've always known it. I just didn't think..."

"Yeah."

"Maybe when things slow down for your family... when they get better..."

Colleen brushed her lips briefly against his and handed him his jacket. "Yeah. Maybe."

Minutes later, the heavy thud of the front door sounded across the house. Colleen sank to the floor and buried her scream in Evangeline's forgotten nightgown.

. . .

CHARLES AWOKE TO THE FIGHT BETWEEN THE SISTERS, first Colleen's shouting, then the inevitable slamming of doors. When the front door opened and closed, he deduced it was over, one way or the other, and went to survey the damage.

Evangeline's door was locked. Her sobs were loud on the other side, but Charles had no idea what to do with those, so he decided not to knock. She was alive. That was about all he was responsible for, anyway.

He didn't dare knock on Colleen's. He wasn't ashamed to say his sister scared him, and he didn't doubt at all that whatever he tried to say in comfort would be woefully inadequate, and that she'd be sure to let him know it.

Charles decided to return to his room, satisfied he'd at least checked on his siblings. When he turned, though, his baby sister stood at the end of the hall, illuminated by the moonlight streaming through the dormer window.

"Lizzy?" He approached her with caution. The uncle of her classmate had died in a construction accident earlier that day.

"Huck," she whispered.

"It's not your fault," he said as he drew closer. "What happened. You know that, right? Predicting something can happen doesn't mean you caused it." When he reached her, she was drenched in sweat. His hands floated above her head and wet nightshift helplessly. He sighed. "We need to get you out of this thing."

"You need to know something, Huck."

"What's that, chicken?" Charles ducked into her room and started rifling through drawers, one at a time. How women organized their clothing was a mystery beyond his understanding or interest.

"Mama is going to pay that girl."

"What girl?" Aha! He reached in and found a blue gown. He tossed it to her and made a twirling motion with his finger. *Put this on. We'll both turn around.*

She caught it but made no move to change. "Shelly."

Charles froze. "What about her?"

"Mama will pay her, Huck, to get rid of that baby. But she won't do it. She'll have the baby anyway, and the baby will be a girl."

His breath sank to his feet. He couldn't have moved if upended by a bulldozer. "No, that's not... Mama is paying her to take care of the problem."

"Yes, but she won't. You're gonna have a daughter, Huck. A little girl. But you'll never meet her as long as you live."

"What..." Charles closed his eyes. "Why are you telling me this?"

"You deserve to know. Mama wants to control everything in our lives, but this time it won't work. You deserve to know you're gonna be a dad."

"A dad." The word didn't sound real even said aloud. He started to ask her if she was sure, but what was the point? What Lizzy saw, happened. Always. This was the burden of being her.

Earlier that day, Irish Colleen had stopped by his room, to tell him it was done. *I paid them handsomely. Way more than the procedure will cost. It'll send that girl to college and hopefully straighten out her life before she tries to ruin another young man's life.*

A little girl. A child, who might have his eyes, or maybe his nose, or even the Deschanel chin. Who might laugh like he did, or approach life with the same gusto. A little girl. *His* little girl.

Elizabeth pulled the fresh nightgown to her chest. "I thought you should know. That's all."

CHAPTER 15

The Measure of a Man

Someone asked Madeline what time it was. She hadn't worn a watch in years, not since she put the little pink Timex her father gave her for her seventh birthday away in her memory box. She thought about telling this random stoner that she didn't even know what *day* it was, let alone the time, but her view for the past week had come with a few lessons. The angle of the sun on the filthy mattress on the far side of the room offered at least a directional answer. No one used that mattress anymore. Not since someone had died on it.

"About dinnertime," she answered. The junkie rolled over, satisfied.

It wasn't just the makeshift sundial, though. Her stomach rumbled on cue. It always rumbled now, when she'd shrugged off her three square meals for whatever she could get her hands on. Someone usually sloughed in around noon with a basket from the local food bank, but the offering was random and inconsistent. One time all they had were a few cans of "meat," bearing indistinct animal shapes as the only clue, and eighteen bags of the sandwich part of ice cream sandwiches.

She'd eaten her share, though.

Yesterday was like Thanksgiving in the drug house, though.

Someone had a brother, or maybe a sister, or maybe not even a relative at all, who worked for McDonald's on Carondelet. Their connection had snuck them all the burgers that had sat past the allowed time, and she came in with a whole bag of them, beaming like Santa Claus with his sack of toys.

The bread was so hard it could have been used to play Frisbee, but it was the best thing Madeline had eaten in days.

Weeks.

It didn't have to be this way. She could go home. Let the hot, clean shower wash away the filth of her failed field trip. Slip on clean clothes, pausing long enough to breathe in the fresh but cloying scent of her mother's Dash laundry detergent. Hell, she'd even be grateful for Colleen's infamous tuna noodle casserole. Maureen's vacuous prattling might sound like Nancy Sinatra after the never-ending bray of police sirens. At some point, so many things that had once been relentless annoyances were tinged with an empty nostalgia.

But going home would be more than a failure. More than admitting her dream of traveling the open road, going from protest to protest, offering her time and heart was not as simple as she'd naively hoped.

It was the night to her day. The thin white line between the life holding her back and the life she was meant to lead. It was LSD versus the white light of making a difference.

Still...

Still.

Madeline closed her eyes as her body jerked forward with each thrust of the man riding her from behind. One hand dug into her hips as he grunted his satisfaction, cigarette dangling precariously over their thin mattress. He hadn't used a rubber, despite her protests, and, come to think of it, hadn't really checked in to see if she wanted this at all.

She didn't. But, he'd given her an extra rock-hard cheeseburger, much to the drooling chagrin of all the other washed up, drug-addled inhabitants of the abandoned house on Tchoupitoulas, and lying quietly while he took his fill, while they all watched her with the sad eyes of those who knew, and would have done the same, was about the cost of it all. Would be the cost of it all as long as he had more stale hamburgers to share.

When he finished, he patted her hip, almost fatherly, and shuffled off to finish his cigarette.

Who said it would be easy to save the world? That there wouldn't be costs?

One day, soon, she'd know her next step. How to emerge from the dregs of this hellhole and get to where she needed to be, where she could make a difference. Where she could give purpose to this curse of caring.

Madeline willed the tears back, back inside, where her hope still lived.

AUGUSTUS HAD SWORN HE'D NEVER USE HIS POWERS OF persuasion for gain, or to shirk responsibility. He'd sworn this so many times, and subsequently broken that promise so many times, that he didn't know if he could rightfully even claim to be a man of his word anymore. If you couldn't be true to yourself, you weren't true at all.

He didn't know if it was worth the effort to even fight it. This was who he was to his family: the Fixer. He was the spare, not the heir, and his usefulness began and ended where his willingness to play along resided. He couldn't see the future like Elizabeth, but it didn't take a soothsayer to know this would be his role, always. No matter what personal and professional accomplishments he might rack up, they would pale beside what he would do for his family to allow them to move about the world without consequence.

Augustus couldn't decide if he was sad or resigned to this fact. He wasn't happy about it, but when had his happiness ever been of any importance to anyone?

Except Madeline. When she wasn't consumed with her insatiable need for philanthropy, she was interested in the things he did and made an authentic attempt to know more. She didn't understand business, but she tried. She asked questions that demonstrated she was listening and not just pretending, like everyone else. She was curious about his decision to open a magazine imprint and was the only person who knew how Augustus loved to read. The only one who knew of his stack of old *New Yorkers* under his bed, with the fascinating shorts and serials. It was important to him, so it was important to her.

In his more cynical moments, he told himself her interest was a byproduct of her empathic senses. That she had no choice but to care.

But he knew better.

Augustus might not be the heir, but he had an intrinsic desire to protect. To provide and care for others. Where he lacked in warmth, he made up for in commitment. His mother, his other siblings, looked for his wisdom, but he had more in him to offer. He wasn't as colorful as Charles, as self-assured as Colleen, as passionate as Madeline, or as smart as Evangeline, as whimsical as Maureen, or as solemn as Elizabeth. Somehow, these traits had come to define them all in ways as important as their name and accomplishments. And Augustus was... he was... just there. Quiet, studious, nothing particularly interesting to offer, at least in their eyes. Until they needed a fixer.

Well, he'd just ensured Charles would never serve a day for his murder of Peter Evers, so he'd more than earned his salt. And why not keep going? Using this "gift" in the dark alleys along the wharf, amongst the abandoned warehouses from another era, as he searched for Madeline. How was it any different than slipping some of these reprobate down-on-their-lucks an Andrew Jackson for the same outcome?

These rationalizations wouldn't make it easier, so he stopped. He had to find Madeline. To suck up his pride and his anger that she'd broken her promise to someone who would have said adherence to a vow was the measure of the man.

Yet how could it be when Augustus was so easily persuaded himself?

Most he talked to had no idea where his sister was. They were incapable of lying when under his sway, so he didn't spend any time separating wheat from chaff. He moved on quickly from place to place, never stopping too long to evaluate his failure.

The Lucky Seven on Girod finally yielded results.

"I think she's with Darko's crew at the old Darbonne house."

"I don't know it."

"Yeah, you don't know it." The clerk, Clyde from his nametag, eyed his pressed suit with as much amusement as the spell allowed. "Down on Tchoup. Keep on down Girod, past the church, until you hit it, and then keep going until you see The Warehouse." He grinned. "You don't know The Warehouse, do you?"

Augustus shook his head, for once in his life wishing he was cooler. He'd heard of the place; an old warehouse where the youth went to hear the Grateful Dead, Fleetwood Mac, and others whom he couldn't name if their music came on the radio. Charles went down there a lot; Madeline had as well.

The clerk laughed. "Head down Tchoup, past St. Mary and past The Warehouse. Just after the bed, you know, before St. Andrew, you'll see the house."

"Which one?" Augustus repeated.

"Well, for one, it's the only house on the block, surrounded by empty warehouses and dockyards. But it's also the only one that ain't got no roof!"

AUGUSTUS WADED THROUGH THE DOWNSTAIRS OF WHAT looked as much part of the outdoors as in. It wasn't only the missing roof—Clyde hadn't been wrong about that—but the wide array of litter decorating what was left of the flooring. The walls had been ripped out at some point, likely for the copper within, and an old couch lay tipped on its side. Someone was passed out against the back of it. His intrusion didn't stir them.

If Madeline had been here... truly been *here,* for the two weeks she'd been missing... he'd never forgive himself. Never.

Or Irish Colleen.

Yes, but you know it. You can feel it. She's here.

Augustus continued. As he moved from room to room, he stopped kicking around the debris in aghast disgust. He was adjusting to his surroundings now, like his pupils when he stepped from the darkness into the light. The shock had worn away, as it always did. Augustus was never out of his element for long.

The oaken bannister was one of the few things still intact. It wound up around the house, which had once been likely very beautiful, revealing a second and possibly third floor. The stairs themselves were another matter. Made of less sturdy material and covered with a thin, faded carpet runner, every few steps had a crater large enough to ruin someone's day.

Augustus unbuttoned his suit coat and ascended.

The upstairs was teeming with life, both human and otherwise. Sleeping young men and young women littered the halls, curled in unnatural positions, some atop each other, too lazy or high to right themselves after a coital tryst. A permanent layer of smoke hung up there, one of mingled scents. Cigarettes, dope, and other things... with a headier scent, one Augustus knew nothing about personally but still recognized. The kind of drugs taken off a hot spoon, or inhaled through a glass pipe.

Evidence of these things, the cast offs of burned broken glass and scorched tinfoil, lay in discarded corners, gathering dust.

A great pit burrowed into his chest. He would say anything—do anything—to get Madeline to come home with him. Anything.

He stumbled from room to room, mostly unnoticed. Those who did curled their lips in bemusement at the well-groomed man who clearly didn't belong. He wanted to scream at them, that none of them did! None of them needed to! That they were nothing without their choices!

But words meant nothing, and his outrage came from a place of privilege many here didn't enjoy. Madeline was undoubtedly the exception, the lone heiress lost in this haze of drugs and forgotten dreams.

Augustus decided in that moment he would donate half his first year's profits to the homeless shelters of New Orleans.

When he found her, lying underneath a middle-aged man, Augustus for the first time in his life had the urge to take a life. He could, like Charles, walk away unscathed if he chose to follow this urge and choke the drug-addled shock right out of the man as the light in his eyes died altogether.

A small butterfly, yellow and blue, caught in mid-flight, fluttered from the outside of Madeline's thigh. His rage shifted to vague, unfocused confusion. He'd never seen that before... but of course he hadn't. The spot was a place of intimacy. And yet, she told him everything. She'd always told him everything. Hadn't she?

He recovered himself and pulled the man off by his arm. He flung him aside, more gently than the man deserved. Madeline didn't jump in surprise, or even react at all. She was half-asleep, her face crusted with layers of tears.

"Dude! That's my girl!"

Augustus started to take a deep breath, then stopped upon realizing this was not air he wanted in his lungs. "No, she's my sister, and you really don't want to be here when I turn around."

The man puffed out a series of affronted protestations, but his voice was already growing distant, and he didn't need to look to see he'd fled.

"Maddy?"

Her eyes blinked open. She licked her dried, cracked lips. "Aggie?"

"Maddy." Augustus pitched forward, weighted by the full power of his emotions. "Thank God I found you. Thank God, thank God, thank God."

"You came for me." She sounded surprised.

"Of course I came for you. Of course," he repeated, over and over. "Of course I came for you."

"I can't go home," she whispered. Her voice, hoarse from lack of use, cracked. "She hates me."

"No, Maddy. She doesn't hate you." Augustus's eyes clouded from the tears. They'd come quickly and with fierce intention. "She is sorry for what she said." *And so am I.* "She misses you so much." *And so do I.*

"Really?"

"Really times a thousand." He didn't want to stay here a moment longer. They could talk about this someplace else, but the longer she stayed here, the more of herself she'd give away. Augustus scooped her thin body into his arms. She smelled ripe with the decay of the place, and the lack of hygiene, but he pressed her into his chest and navigated the house with the urgent purpose of a firefighter pulling someone from a raging fire.

When he got her outside, she cried out from the sun. How long had it been since she'd been outside at all? He couldn't ask. Some things hurt too much to know.

"I can't go back," she choked out between her tears. "I love you, but I can't."

"I know," Augustus replied through his own tears, and he did. He did know. He'd been thinking about this throughout this whole search, and whatever his goals, his dreams, they could wait until after she was safe. "I'll protect you."

"I know you want to, but you can't, Aggie. You have your own life."

"My life will be there, Maddy. It's not going anywhere. I'll get you through this last year of high school and give you anything you need when you graduate. Anything in the world. Anything you want. I'll even drive you to wherever you want to go. I'll tell Mom... I'll tell her, I'm your parent now. She has to come through me, and she can't yell at you. She's not allowed. And if she does... if she does, Maddy, I'll get us our own place until you're out of school, okay? I'll do *anything* to get you through this next year. You just need to graduate and then I'll help you go where you wanna go. I'll pay your way the rest of your life. All of it."

Madeline sobbed against his chest. He held her in his firm grip, unsure if the words were right, even if they were true. His promise was irrational, but to lose his sister would be akin to a death of the part of himself that still held onto the occasional optimism. What little of him saw the value in idealism. She was a mirror and reflected back a purpose bigger than what everyone else asked of him, or even what he asked of himself.

"You don't have to do so much for me."

"It's not so much, really." He exhaled into her filthy hair. His breath hitched. Augustus suspected he would never know what it was like to fall in love, and that was okay. There were other kinds of love. To save someone who needed you was the most powerful kind of love there was. "It feels like almost nothing, to know you'll be safe."

"What if I fail you?" Her lips quivered, and she looked so young, so vulnerable.

"No," he said. "No, you could never. *I* failed *you,* and it won't happen again."

"That's not true. I should have listened to you."

"It doesn't matter, Maddy." He kissed her dirty forehead, cutting through the grease. "You're coming home now, and none of that matters."

MADELINE WAS SWALLOWED WHOLE BEFORE THE DOOR was halfway open. Her mother, sisters, even Charles, swarmed around her, enveloping her in forgiveness and love, love without judgment, the family she'd been born into and survived; the family she'd suffered through, and ultimately left.

Her family.

Through a crack in the swell of arms and faces, she watched Augustus climb the stairs, gripping the bannister as if no longer able to carry his own weight.

She could do this. For him, she could do it.

WINTER 1970

NEW ORLEANS, LOUISIANA

CHAPTER 16

But Then What?

Colin Sullivan sat across from Charles at Giraud's Pub. He didn't look as surprised as he should.

Long sigh. "The truth is, Charles I knew."

Charles threw his hands up. "You knew?" Of course he knew. Rory knew and had been using that information to try and win Colleen back, which was a lost cause if Charles ever saw one. His sister was the ice queen on ice steroids, and she couldn't kick that habit any more than Charles could kick the China White. She didn't even talk to her best friend Carolina anymore. Or any of her siblings, for that matter.

"Dad has me on a part-time internship at the firm." In contrast to Charles' aggressive gesturing, Colin looked ready to retreat. "Your mom used us to complete the payoff and the contract. When I overheard, Dad told me I had to practice attorney-client privilege and keep it to myself. In this case, your mom was the client."

"And I'm your best friend and, oh, that's right, the fucking heir! I outrank my mom, punk."

Another sigh from his long-suffering best friend. "That's a two-way street, Charles. You could have come to me, too. You didn't."

Charles sputtered through a few more obscenities before he said, "Well, I'm here now."

"You know as much as I do," Colin said.

"Tell me what the fuck you know and then I'll confirm whether that's true."

Colin shrugged. "Honestly, I don't know much. I know her name is Shelly Cointreau. Seeing as I don't know anyone by that name, you already know more than I do."

"Go on, man. What else?"

Colin's eyes darted around. "Um, well… they're from Algiers, but after the payout they moved out of state. Don't know where. Shelly's just a kid."

"I did *not* fucking know that salient fact when she was riding me into the eclipse."

Colin closed his eyes. "Gross. And anyway, I believe you. Even you have standards."

"Did I tell you I think I was raped, man? That's what it means, right, when someone has sex with you and you don't even know it's happening?"

"Yes, if that's what happened."

"It is!"

"Fine." Colin raised his hands. "That's what happened."

"What else?"

"The payoff was a quarter million dollars."

"The fuck?"

"Irish Colleen really wanted to make this go away," Colin replied. "She made that clear. She asked what it would take. That was the number they gave." He shook his head with a laugh. "If only they knew they could have added a zero and she would've still paid it."

"Well, it didn't go away, Colin."

"Maybe Elizabeth is wrong."

Charles glared at him. Elizabeth was never wrong.

"Fine. Okay. She's not wrong. What are you hoping to get out of this?"

"Get out of this?" Charles boomed. "Get out? I'm going to be a father, Colin!"

Colin leaned in and opened his eyes wide. "And unless you want all of Uptown to know, I suggest keeping it down."

"That's the most helpful advice you've offered. Can you help me with something more important now?"

"You didn't answer my question, Charles. What do you want from this? Don't yell at me, I want you to really think before you answer. Do you want to raise this child with Shelly? Take her from her mother?"

Charles recoiled. "Are those my only choices?"

"I suppose there are others, but... look, the contract specified Shelly had to abort the child in order for her family to accept the money. Of course, that sort of language is easily disputed in court, because you can't accept a bribe for what equates, legally, to murder, but—"

"Do I give a shit? Fuck my mother's payoff. I have access to far more money than she could wish up in her wildest dreams. I jack off with more cash than she has in her bank account."

Colin winced. "Not until you're twenty-one."

"I'm twenty, nimrod. We're practically dancing in that backyard."

"And yet, you *still* haven't given me a direct answer."

Charles fell back against the peeling plastic seat. What he wanted... well, who the fuck knew what he wanted? What he *knew* was there would very, very soon, any day now if his math wasn't a complete waste, be a little girl in the world who was half his. A baby Charles. Charlotte was a nice name. And what else did he have? Everything, if you looked at it from one point of view. Nothing, from another. The yawning void separating Charles from his siblings had become too far to vault across. This hadn't started when he murdered that pedophile teacher, but it sped things along, for sure. And now, nothing was okay. Something had to change... to make it all right again.

"Does it matter?"

"Where this is concerned, yes," Colin said, "it matters."

"I want an address."

"No."

"You're my attorney!"

"No, I'm your best friend. But your attorney would tell you part of the agreement was sealing their contact information, probably to avoid this very situation. Shelly Cointreau, previously from Algiers. That's all you'll ever get, Charles. I'm sorry."

"If this was your child, you wouldn't be so flip about it, Colin."

"It wouldn't be my child, because I don't get wasted and have sex with strangers at parties."

Charles cracked his knuckles. "If you were anyone else..."

Colin rolled his eyes. "You'd what?"

Charles eased back a bit. "Since you're not my attorney, as you said, you can help me."

Colin shook his head. "It doesn't work like that. The files are redacted. I couldn't get her address even if I wanted to. Her mother mentioned moving up north somewhere, New England I think, and she was going to change her name and give Shelly her maiden name. I don't know her maiden name, and I suspect Cointreau wasn't a real name, either, truth be told. They don't want to be found."

"That's a start."

"It's a dead end."

"Why aren't you on my side?"

Colin paused before answering. "Did you ever stop to think that when I'm telling you what you don't want to hear, that *this* is when I am *most* on your side?"

"I don't even know what you just said."

"I know you're pissed at your mother," Colin said. He slowed his words, something he reserved for when he was especially trying to get his point across. "I know you're thinking about a child out there that shares your DNA and maybe looks like you. I would be, too."

Charles pounded the rest of his beer and ordered another.

"But sometimes.... Sometimes life works out the way it's supposed to. Maybe Shelly is better off. And maybe you are too, Charles."

"Better off?" Charles repeated the words with a scowl, like poison in his mouth. "How could my child be better off with someone else?"

"Her mother. That someone else is her mother."

"And she has more right to our daughter than I do?"

"Legally, yeah, she probably will."

"Legally, this won't even make it to court because all the judges are in my pocket."

Colin exhaled. He signaled for the check. "This is going nowhere. I'd encourage you to think, *really* think, about this. About whether you really want this. I'm sure a decent private detective could get ahold of enough of a paper trail of records to find them, but then what?" He dropped a ten on the slip of paper.

"Where the fuck do you think you're going?"

Colin smiled for the first time in their conversation. "There's this girl."

"A girl! Since when?"

His friend checked his watch. "We met a couple weeks ago at a fundraiser for heart disease. My mother dragged me along, and... I gotta go. I'm gonna be late in meeting her. I'll introduce you to her soon, I promise."

"You fucking better!" Charles exclaimed. He couldn't believe it. Colin Sullivan had a girlfriend. Finally. "What's her name?" he called after him.

Colin threw his blazer over one shoulder and grinned. "Catherine. Catherine Connelly. But she goes by Cat."

CHAPTER 17

Through the Chasm

Maureen spent a lot of her time wondering what would finally, ultimately be what broke the Deschanels. With each and every new scandal or drama, she'd think, ah, this, *this* is what will finally push us all through the chasm. Instead, each thing just peeled one more finger from the edge.

There weren't many fingers left.

Nineteen seventy had been one hell of a year.

She moved about her first year in high school with a level of disinterest impressive even for her. Maureen had never enjoyed school, and her goals didn't require her to be much of a student—trophy wife was an IQ-agnostic job. With the dangling promise of a life with Peter now shattered, though, she'd determined to at least try to pass her classes. Unlike that drama queen Madeline, Maureen accepted a diploma was something one must get regardless of one's aspirations, unless one wished to be branded a failure. And with no backup plan to her dream of being Mrs. Evers, Maureen possessed a pragmatism, however mild, that would have impressed even Colleen.

It was this general understanding of what was required of her that prompted Maureen to start thinking more about how she could accomplish this. There was no way, no how, she could get through high school with the ghost of Peter Evers brooding over her shoulder with his pathetic, "Why, Maureen?" every few minutes.

"You know why!" she snapped today. Maureen had managed not to respond to his pitiful recitations throughout all of fall, but coming into Christmas, her patience was so thin she could snap it with a sneeze. Between Madeline's stunt at the drug house—which now meant everyone had to walk on eggshells around the little princess, lest she run off with yet another drug dealer—Colleen's extreme bitchiness, Evangeline's attention grabs by not ever coming out of her room, and Elizabeth *yet again* having to switch schools, she'd had about enough.

Peter's sad, vacant eyes implored her. "Why, Maureen?"

"Because you can't fuck a fourteen-year-old without consequences, you old creeper!" she cried out, and really, truly, she would've never said such a thing if she'd remembered she was in the middle of Health class.

Oops.

Worse, even, than her mother having to come get her at school was the realization that what she said to Mr. Evers was true. She even believed it now. He *was* a creeper. What kind of man turns to a child for what he should be getting from a woman? Maureen couldn't fault him for cheating on his wife. She obviously wasn't giving him what he needed if he'd turned elsewhere. But with a child? Maureen was no ordinary child, clearly, if she could attract the eyes of a mature man, but this was less about her charms and more about a sickness within him.

She wondered often if her slow acceptance of this fact was her way of trying to live with what Charles did. What Colleen and Augustus helped to cover up. His death was tied to her fractured relationship to almost half her family, and over time, the sting had softened, but the bonds remained fractured.

It wasn't as if she was ever close to any of them, but now she felt apart in a more profound way. Apart with a capital A-P-A-R-T.

Maureen was doing well at neither family nor school, and in a rare moment of wisdom, decided that to achieve her goals she needed to improve at both.

After twenty of her classmates observed her outburst to a ghost, she wasn't sure she should go back. She had an idea, though Mama wouldn't like it.

"You can't leave, Sweet Maureen."

"Hell's bells, Daddy!" She clutched her chest. She'd been sitting alone in her room, working up the courage to have the conversation with her mother. They were the only ones home, after Maureen's mid-day field trip home.

"If you leave, I can't come with you."

Oh? In that case, I'll go today! "I know, Daddy." Her brief spurt of anger faded to sadness at the idea. She hated that she could see him. She missed him so much that she craved these moments. Madness, further and further into madness. The point of no return was coming.

"You're my only connection to this world, my sweet girl. If I could have seen the future and known… I might have let the healers heal me. Your mother needs me. I see that now."

Maureen rolled her eyes. She spat her gum at the canister in the corner and missed. The white wad hit the floor and settled next to the baseboard heater. "A little too late, dontcha think?"

"We're always too late when it matters," he said, sighing. "I know why you want to go. But this family cannot be divided. Who you are is a secret to the rest of the world, but not each other."

"Might as well be a secret here, for all we're allowed to talk about it!"

August hung his head. "I failed to adequately prepare your mother to handle this alone."

"Ya think, Dick Tracy?"

"I may be dead, but don't you mouth off to me, Maureen."

"Sorry." She wanted to laugh. Apologizing to a ghost. Yelling at a ghost. She talked to ghosts more than the living!

"Your mother needs you. Madeline needs you. Colleen needs you."

"Colleen needs no one but her own damn self."

"That's not true and you know it."

Maureen twisted her mouth into a pout. "They might need me more if they realized what it was like to miss me," she said and hopped off the bed. "Here goes nothing."

IT WAS OVER BEFORE SHE COULD GET THE REMAINDER OF the sentence out.

"Boarding school? Have you lost your mind?"

Yes. "Mama, I hate it there! I need a new start. Somewhere I can focus and not be distracted." She stood behind her mother in the kitchen.

"Distracted by what? Boys? They have those in boarding school, too, you know."

If only she knew. Boys. Maureen had only known men. "Not boys, Mama. Everything else."

"Everything else isn't very specific, Maureen." She dropped her dust rag. Leaned over the kitchen sink, eyes trained out the window. "What makes you think leaving here will make you less distracted?"

Maureen had never had the urge to tell her mother about her terrible ability until now. But she couldn't, not now or ever. "I don't know, I just do."

"Not good enough," replied Irish Colleen, who returned to dusting the ledge behind the sink. Dismissed.

"So is you saying no without even thinking about it!" Maureen cried.

Irish Colleen's arms went stiff as she gripped the sink. She made no sigh, but Maureen felt it just the same. "I'm not sending you away just because you want a new adventure. And, with everything that's happened, it's important we all stay close. Together, as a family."

Maureen slammed her fist into the wood hutch. A massive wall of pain nearly blinded her. The damn thing was oak. "Don't punish us all just because Madeline is a drug-addled whore!"

The words were out, and she wished she could take them back. She didn't even mean them. Madeline was a lot of things, but not those things.

"Maureen... Amelia... Deschanel."

They both turned at the sound of a cry in the hall. Irish Colleen blew past Maureen, knocking her aside, as she went after the sobbing Madeline.

"She didn't mean it, Maddy! Your sister didn't mean it!"

"I did," Maureen lied, crying herself now. It was a mess, all of it. All of them. A mess with no cure. Apologies were weak bandages.

Upstairs, a door slammed. She was used to the sound now and didn't even jump. Doors slamming was a pretty regular occurrence in the Deschanel house these days.

Irish Colleen's soft features were a mix of hardness and hatred. "You go apologize to her, Maureen. I don't care if you mean it. You tell Madeline you're sorry, and that you love her, or I will... I will..."

She didn't finish.

MADELINE RESISTED THE URGE TO FLEE TO HER brother's room, to tell him what happened. He would comfort her, of course. He'd been more than good on his word to protect her, and Irish Colleen had fallen in line, too. Whatever she really thought, she hid it well and treated Madeline with a softness she'd never known from her mother. She wished only that she knew if this was real, or her fears manifested through a series of programmed motions.

She'd lived up to her part. Her grades weren't going to get her on any lists, but they were enough. Enough was all she'd promised, and she couldn't let Augustus down. Not now.

Five months. That's all she had to survive. Five months, and she'd walk down that aisle in her cap and gown, collect that worthless piece of paper that meant so much to her dearest brother, and then he'd send her to D.C. She hadn't told him that's where she wanted to go, but she'd already decided. He was going to dip into the trust fund money that all Deschanels collected at twenty-one, but had access to earlier if in college, and she would pay him back every last cent when she turned twenty-one. Whatever Augustus did for her, she would do back, a hundredfold.

Mostly, she would make him proud. Her letters home would ease his heart and show him that a life of activism was not only as good as a career, but better. He would see how happy she was, and... at peace.

She just had to make it to May.

Madeline had promised to graduate. She hadn't promised anything about how she'd get there.

She dialed the numbers on the rotary phone in the hall.

Charles sat on the couch. His hands ached from being cuffed. For once, he was glad not to be high, because he was not the slickest about hiding it. Not that he ever bothered to practice. Who would do anything about it?

Except the police, who were parked in his living room.

Red and blue lights colored the night sky outside. Two in the morning, and the neighborhood was lit up like the Christmas tree of law enforcement. No doubt the neighbors were pissed to high hell. Fuck 'em.

The rest of the room was about as far from the Norman Rockwell Christmas painting as a family could get.

Madeline, red faced and huddled under Augustus' coat in the corner.

Irish Colleen, hair still in rollers, alternating between underbreath curses and full-on Irish outbursts.

Colleen and Augustus, standing sentry on either side of the room, arms both crossed, like mirror-imaged dark angels.

The youngest three had been banished upstairs, but he knew good and well they were crowded near the bannister, straining to hear. It was what he would have done.

The ambulance pulled away moments ago. Inside was Madeline's boyfriend—or drug dealer, Charles didn't fucking know, but he was twice her age, and that was not something he'd abide under any moniker—who used to have a decent face but now wore hamburger in its place. As they strapped him to the gurney, Irish Colleen demanded he apologize. He laughed instead.

He was not the least bit sorry for knocking the dog shit out of that piece of ass like the rented mule he was. Coming around here when Madeline was trying to pull her life together.

Fuck. That.

"Let's start from the beginning, Charles."

"Mr. Deschanel," Charles corrected. "We're not friends."

The officer in charge swung his head as if to say, *Have it your way.* "Mr. Deschanel, let's start from the beginning."

"Officer, it's very late," Irish Colleen said, voice heavy. "My children are very tired. Can we do this tomorrow? I'll bring him down first thing."

"We can do this here or at the station, Mrs. Deschanel, but we're doing it tonight. That man just left in an ambulance."

She waved her hand and buried her sniffling nose in a monogrammed handkerchief.

Augustus and Colleen exchanged looks across the room. Augustus heaved forward in disgust and stepped between the officers and Charles.

"We're done here. Charles was defending himself. We're paying the hospital bills for Bill, or whatever his name is. Good?"

Both officers nodded and put their notebooks back in their shirt pocket. They apologized to Irish Colleen, and then to the rest of the family, and finally un-cuffed Charles before excusing themselves.

The sound of their radios trailing into the night was all that could be heard in the Deschanel living room.

Augustus stormed off in disgust. Madeline started after him, but Colleen held a hand up.

"He's not mad at you, Maddy. He's mad at me."

"Why did you make him do that?" Madeline sobbed. "He

thinks you all only love him for what he can do for you! Don't you know that?"

"Stuff and nonsense," Irish Colleen said. Her voice skittered with light sobs. "We all do what we have to do to protect the family."

"Is that what you call this?" She gestured around the dysfunctional scene. "Who's gonna protect us from ourselves?"

"Oh, shut the fuck *up,*" Charles boomed. He shot to his feet. His wrists were jelly. "Madeline, you of all people have some real nerve pointing fingers."

"Charles," Colleen cautioned.

"You're not Mother Theresa, Colleen. You're not Mother *Anyone,* last time I checked."

"Billy wasn't hurting *anyone*, Huck. But you can't handle anyone having fun that you haven't approved!" Madeline shrugged off the jacket and launched herself at him. "And you can use that 'you of all people' line on yourself next, brother. We all know you did something terrible last summer, and Augustus saved your ass."

"What?" Irish Colleen whipped her head around.

"Nothing, Mama," Charles hissed with a hard look at Madeline. "I'm a goddamn mess, and that's no secret, but ever wonder why all the drama in this household points back to you?"

"That's not fair," Madeline cried. "Or true." She looked pleadingly at Colleen for help, but their sister's gaze was fixed to her feet.

"Look at our mother!" He ran his hands over Irish Colleen's hair, coiled in curlers. "Look at that gray! That's you, Maddy! You! You stupid, ungrateful bitch, *you* are sending our mother to an early grave!"

Madeline fled the room in tears.

Irish Colleen ripped the pins from her hair, one by one, and threw them at her son. "You! Don't! Speak! For! Me!"

Soon, she was gone, too.

"You shouldn't have said that," Colleen said. She rolled his hands over in hers, passing her healing to him. The broken skin fused back together. The redness ebbed. How many times had she healed his indiscretions? "You really shouldn't have said that."

"Better check on that nosebleed, sister," Charles accused. He regarded both hands, now pristine, and shook her away. He should thank her, but he didn't. He never did. Her role in the family was healer, just as his was to lead. "Awfully elevated there on your high horse."

"I stood by you last summer. You did what you had to do. But this?" She gestured toward the stairs, where every last one of the Deschanels had fled the scene in one form or another, except them. "You went too far, and what's worse is you know it. You know it, and you'll never apologize, because you're the *heir* and you think that somehow places you in the pecking order just south of God."

Moments later, Charles found himself alone in the parlor, with only their string of accusations and one hell of a headache.

CHAPTER 18

We Are Not Partners

The Deschanel Magi Collective Council met quarterly as a matter of protocol. Twice annually for the broader Collective. The frequency increased only in their times of great need. A good year had no more than the standard four and two.

Despite the turmoil in Colleen's own household, this was a rare moment of peace for her family as a whole. As the final Council meeting of 1970 came to a close, in the earliest hours of December 24, and Kitty Guidry filed away their notes, Colleen took only small comfort in this peace.

The Gardens was lit ceiling to floor with white lights. Garland wrapped around bannisters and columns, while brilliant shades of red and pink blossomed with the hundreds of poinsettias, small and large. A tree fit for a more public affair stood sentry at the bay window facing Jackson Avenue, for all the passersby to see. Everyone in Uptown waited for the Deschanel Tree to go up in the window so they could take their children by the hand and point at the splendor.

Colleen said goodbye to her cousins, one by one. Most were headed for a brief rest and then off to some family affair or another. Christmas was a holiday like no other for Deschanels, Broussards,

Fontenots, and all the many other branches down their lines. A time for joy and ceremony.

Aunt Ophelia's frail hand squeezed hers as they stood in the doorway and watched the others file away, returning to the dark night and their own lives.

"You seem in no hurry to follow," Ophelia wheezed. She coughed into the sleeve of her green satin smoking jacket. Colleen steadied her until she was finished.

"How could you tell?"

"With age comes wisdom." She coughed a gravelly laugh. "Or finer observation skills."

Colleen pressed her body into the heavy double doors to close them. "I don't think I've ever felt so lost, Aunt Ophelia."

Ophelia took her niece's arm. "That's a feeling as predictable as death and taxes. One you'll feel many times over your life, and when you think you've felt it enough, you'll feel it again."

Colleen steered them toward the back porch overlooking the generous gardens for which the property was named. Crepe myrtle and bird of paradise lorded over the luscious space. It had always been a retreat of safeness for Colleen. Where everything came together, and all was right.

"I wish it were so simple."

"Shall we waste time having you recant the past couple months of your life, my dearest, or will you allow me to stop pretending I don't already know?"

Colleen couldn't help but laugh. "I know you know, Tante. And I was hoping you might have some of your famous wisdom for me."

"Wisdom or divination?"

She considered this before answering. "Mostly wisdom. Maybe a touch of the other."

Ophelia eased down into her rocker with some aid from Colleen. The cicadas were loud tonight, louder than usual for the winter, but this time of year they faced no competition. "The Deschanels will come out of this, as they always do."

"In one piece?"

Ophelia waved her hand back and forth. "You asked only for a touch of divination, my dear."

"I don't know how to help my family anymore."

"Do you mean your brother being a murderer? Or your sister a victim of an older man? There are other transgressions and sins, I know, but we can begin there."

Colleen was shocked. "You know about those things?"

Ophelia's wrinkled mouth curled in a smile. "Don't insult me, child."

"My mother doesn't know." Colleen slumped in her chair. She exhaled, watching the swirl of breath dance on the night sky. "About either thing. She can never know."

"She never will," Ophelia replied. "And yes, that is divination. You can thank me, for taking that burden from your shoulders."

Colleen twisted her hands in her lap. "Good. I think it would kill her."

"Your mother is far stronger than you give her credit for."

"Just the same."

"Do you think it is you, Colleen, who must protect your mother from the ills of the world?"

"No—"

"No, not to me. You won't lie to me," Ophelia said. "I'm weary tonight, child. Wish I could stay up into the sunrise with you. But my old body no longer supports the whims of my mind. Shall we get to the advice you sought so dearly?"

Colleen nodded.

"What you desire is wisdom, but what you need most is to make peace with your anger."

"My anger?"

"At your siblings. At the world. At yourself," Ophelia answered. "You carry it like an old, expensive handbag you're too stubborn to discard."

"That's not fair," Colleen began. "You don't know—"

"I do know, and I'm tired, so let's cease with the interruptions.

You must learn to forgive and move on, before it's too late. Nothing has been done that cannot be forgiven, Colleen. Your family needs you, though not in the way you seem to want to believe. They need you to be their daughter and their sister. Their friend. There will come a time in your life when your authority will be the more pressing need, but that day is not today. It is not tomorrow, either." Ophelia pitched forward and wrapped her bony hand around Colleen's knee. "When the time comes, you will know. I promise. But it's Christmas, and there is no better occasion for good old-fashioned forgiveness, would you not agree?"

Colleen nodded through her tears. She'd gotten what she came for, but she wasn't confident her aunt was on the mark this time. She'd lived many years, maybe too many, and the length might be diluting the content.

"Thank you, Tante," she whispered and kissed her aunt good night.

"Thank me by enjoying this Christmas with your family," Ophelia replied, and Colleen was left feeling as if there was a second half to the sentence left unspoken.

IRISH COLLEEN WAITED FOR HER ON THE COUCH IN THE parlor.

Colleen leaned forward and kissed her cheek. "You didn't have to wait up, Mama."

"I always wait up after your meetings."

"I know, but I'm an adult now. I'll be all right."

"Just the same." Irish Colleen looped her fingers through the knits of her shawl. "You were later than usual tonight."

"I spent some time with Aunt Ophelia," Colleen said. "I don't get much time with her anymore."

Her mother nodded, her face unreadable in the dim light. "Did she have good advice for you?" They both knew the old woman was the only person Colleen ever solicited or digested advice from.

"She thinks I'm holding onto anger," Colleen said. She told the truth before she thought too much about whether she should. "That instead I should learn to forgive."

Irish Colleen cracked a smile. "There's wisdom in the old bat yet. And did you find this advice helpful?"

"I found it confusing," Colleen said, continuing her streak of stark honesty. "I don't think she's wrong, but I don't know that she understands, either. She hasn't been here this year, experiencing everything we've all experienced."

"Sometimes an outside opinion can help put things in perspective."

"You agree with her? You think I'm angry?"

Irish Colleen shrugged with her hands out. "I think you carry more than you should. If it's anger, that's between you and God."

"God," Colleen said. "Anger is a sin in his eyes."

"So is deception, even when the person you're deceiving is yourself."

"What are you talking about?"

"Colleen, you speak to me as if we're equals most of the time. As if you think it's your responsibility to raise this family. Just the other day you asked me what 'we' were going to do about Madeline. My child, 'we' are not going to do anything. I'm going to pray for guidance while you focus on getting your education, and God willing, both will work out in the end."

Colleen was speechless. Of course she knew she wasn't an equal with her mother. "I'm trying to help you! I know you've had it hard since Daddy died, and there's seven of us and one of you. I stepped up when no one else would."

"You stepped up when no one asked," Irish Colleen said, direct but gentler than usual, as if she understood it was needed.

"That's not fair!" she cried, for the second time that night.

"It's life, which has never been fair," her mother replied. "We're not partners, Colleen. When you act like we are, it doesn't relieve my stress, it adds to it."

"How am I adding to your stress?"

"All I've ever wanted was to see you seven happy and healthy.

And all of you, right now, are sick, and I don't know if prayer is enough. Yes, even you, Leena. Your sickness is you're not able to live your life. God help me for saying this, but I used to *wish* you'd go to parties! Unlike Charles, or even your sisters, who I've always had to rein in, I thought, if only you could do normal things with your friends, maybe, just maybe..."

"Just maybe what?"

Irish Colleen suppressed a yawn and pulled herself to her feet. "I don't say this often, but you should listen to that old woman. Sometimes she gets it right. You do need to let go, and you need to forgive, starting with yourself."

"I don't know what to say."

Irish Colleen kissed the top of her head. "Merry Christmas, Colleen. Sleep and think of a way to make yourself happy."

CHAPTER 19

Dream a Little Dream of Me

The veins in Augustus' neck strained so tight he wondered if it was possible for them to pop. If they did, would they spray blood everywhere? He supposed if his carotid artery went, that would be the end of that, but he might survive the destruction of a lesser vein.

His most effective method of stress moderation had always come in the form of making a conscious decision to not let things get to him. He told Colleen this once, and was met with the forehead bulging incredulity he expected. The girl who carried the stress of the world couldn't fathom just *deciding* things didn't bother her.

But it worked. Where Charles and the girls got spun up about every last thing, Augustus was able to focus on those things in life that would move him forward, not pull him back. School had never been a problem, and his goals were clear. He loved his family, even if they weren't exactly the Cleavers.

This moderated approach to life was why he'd been the best equipped to weather Madeline's storms. She could cry, scream, throw things, and he never matched her pique, never rose to her level of outrage. He thought, just maybe, this was what she needed most. Someone who could listen and be there without being just like her.

The stint in the drug house changed all that. Every faded smile was a warning sign. Smart-ass comments between sisters could send everything in his unsteady house of cards crashing to the floor in pieces. And he'd promised her. He'd sworn a vow that what she was coming back to was safe.

But it wasn't, because even when everything changes, nothing does.

First, he'd watched Maureen hurl a plate at Madeline's head when Madeline made an offhand comment about "that warmonger Nixon." Maureen, who hadn't the faintest head for politics, declared that she was "done, just done, and tell Mama she can take her allowance away because she can't do what she asked anymore."

As it turned out, what Irish Colleen had asked was for Maureen to hold her tongue around Madeline, and the reward was double the usual five dollars. Augustus later learned she'd tried to bribe the other kids as well, with varying levels of success.

Charles went out of his way to ignore Madeline, and when they were forced into close quarters, like at dinnertime, his avoidance was so obvious it put a finer point on his anger than an outburst would have. Instead, that bomb just ticked, ticked, ticked, magnifying the inevitable blast radius.

Evangeline retreated into her own world, more so even than usual, flashing only occasionally guilty looks at her older sister that she never explained. Something had happened between them, but neither was talking.

Only Elizabeth held onto a genuine compassion for her sister. Wordless, she'd cling to Madeline everywhere she went, or follow her, offering help with menial tasks like carrying her laundry basket, and even folding and putting away the clothes. She tidied her room, and one day left flowers on her dresser. This was all very curious when Elizabeth's room looked post-apocalyptic unless Mama decided to surrender and clean it for her.

Instead of being a comfort, this inexplicable shift in Elizabeth's behavior only left Augustus feeling more unsteady. And he could see it was doing the same to Madeline.

Everything came to a crashing conclusion in the early morning hours of Christmas Eve.

Colleen had come in late from her Council meeting. On her way up to bed, Madeline tried to say something to her. Augustus never heard what it was, because he only woke up to the aftermath.

"I don't know anything about that part of your life. I'm just trying to take an interest in what you do," Madeline defended. These were the first clear words Augustus heard.

"Since when!" shrieked Colleen, and that's when he knew this was headed nowhere fast.

"Since now, I guess," Madeline said. By then, Maureen had spilled into the hall, moments before Augustus. "We're sisters, Colleen."

"Sisters," Colleen repeated. Augustus could see she'd been crying. Whatever caused her distress, it began before she'd ever ascended the steps. "Right. A little late for that, isn't it, Maddy? Now you want to be sisters? I've been here all along, where have you been?"

"Come *on*," Charles growled. He stumbled out in his boxers, rubbing sleep from his eyes. "Do you assholes know what time it is?"

"I'm trying," Madeline pleaded. "I'm not like you."

Colleen laughed. The callous sound was nothing like her, and Augustus was concerned for them both then. "Trying looks a little different in your world, doesn't it?"

"Colleen..."

"Leena, stop." Elizabeth's small voice called from down the hallway. "Don't."

Augustus pulled up behind Colleen and tried to whisper in her ear. To get her to stand down. But whatever had affected Colleen had taken over. Later, he wondered—many, many times—if he had broken their family rule and got into her head to stop her, would things have been different?

"Why did you even come back, Madeline? For food? Shelter?" Colleen swung her hands around the hall, now filled with all seven of the Deschanel children. "You've never hesitated to make sure we know just how much you hate us all. Your complete and utter *disdain* for what we stand for. So don't call me sister when we both know you're using that word as a means to an end that has nothing to do with kinship."

"Hey, hey," Charles started, coming toward them both with a hand in the air. "Come on, let's all just get to bed."

Evangeline pulled Elizabeth into her side when the little girl burst into tears.

"That's awful rich coming from someone who can't even hold on to her boyfriend because she's so cold and dead inside." When Madeline threw this punch back, Augustus knew it was over.

All of it.

Every last thing he'd tried to do, and any progress made with it.

Colleen laughed through her stuttered speech. "Dead inside? If I'm dead it's from the stress of watching you throw your life away! It's from watching you suck the life from our mother. You weren't here, Madeline! You didn't see our mother's hair graying and her sleepless nights. Why? Because *you only ever think of yourself!*"

"Colleen, the exact *opposite* of that is true. I am who I am because I'm incapable of thinking of myself first. Don't you think I'd be happier that way?"

Colleen pointed at her. Her arm trembled in the socket and the finger bobbed up and down, up and down, a buoy of accusation. "I don't think you'll be happy until the world burns around you and you're the goddamn glowing center of it all."

Madeline blew past her sister, past the others, a blur of wavy hair and pajamas flying down the stairs.

"What have you done?" Augustus demanded before running after her. He didn't stay to wait for the answer.

. . .

THE BUS STATION WAS EMPTY AT THIS HOUR.

Evangeline showed up with the bag an hour after they arrived. He'd felt bad dragging her across New Orleans at this godforsaken hour, and on Christmas Eve, but who else could he ask? He was grateful it had been her, and not one of the others, who answered when he called from the payphone.

"Yeah, well, there's zero chance of hitting rapid eye movement sleep after that Broadway show," Evangeline said and put up no fight when Augustus made his request. He only hoped she'd packed the bag sensibly enough, though the cash he slipped into Madeline's jacket pocket should more than compensate for any oversight.

"Thanks, Evie," he said and took the bag.

"Thank me by paying the cab. I don't have any cash, hombre."

Augustus slipped outside and took care of the bill. When he returned, he told her to wait and he'd take her home with him. One dicey taxi was enough for the night. He'd already have an earful when Irish Colleen woke in the morning to the aftermath of his decision.

"She's really leaving, then? For real this time?"

Augustus nodded. He slipped an arm over her shoulder. "I'm out of better ideas. She can't stay here."

"No," she agreed.

"Do *you* have a better idea?"

"Not really." Evangeline chewed her lip. Several raw spots betrayed the trail of carnage, and she sucked on the resulting blood. "Hey, look, you need to tell her Colleen didn't mean that. She can't leave thinking that."

"I already did," he said. "She knows, but..." *It doesn't matter,* he almost said, but it did. He'd spent his short life convincing himself not to sweat the details, but he knew better now; that every spoken word left a mark, for better or worse.

"Colleen will never forgive herself for it."

"She should. We've all done things, and said things, we shouldn't."

"Well, she won't."

Augustus sighed. "I know. Hey, I need to have a few words with Maddy, in private." He pulled out his leather wallet and slipped her a few dollars. "Go hit up that vending machine and park next to the magazine rack, okay? I won't be long."

Evangeline held her hand out and blinked hard a few times. He laughed and handed her more money.

"Mama will *kill* me if she knows I'm eating after midnight," Evangeline said with undisguised glee. Her combat boots echoed like gunfire as she skipped toward defiance.

Augustus found Madeline looking through the bag. "She did okay. Evangeline."

"Good. You can buy whatever you need when you get there."

"I don't need much."

He tucked her hair behind her ear. "I know."

"I know you hate this, Aggie."

"This," he said. "But not you."

"You did everything you could. Everything you promised. Sometimes things just don't work out."

He wasn't so sure, but what she needed, on the verge of this new life, were reassurances. "Everything is going to be okay."

Madeline kissed the corner of his mouth. "You're the only reason I tried as hard as I did. You deserve to be happy, too, Aggie. Don't let them use you, or tell you who you are. Find someone who will love you for the best parts."

He laughed. "I'm not even thinking about that right now, Maddy."

She mussed his hair. "But you will, you dope. You will."

Augustus looked around. Though there was no one else but the three of them, that made it somehow worse. A void. "I don't like the idea of leaving you here until morning."

"Don't be a doofus. My friends will be here soon."

"Maybe I should wait until they arrive."

"Nonsense," Madeline insisted, and she made it sound like exactly that. "You're going to go home and get some sleep, and in the morning you'll register for spring term and get things back on track."

"Okay, Mom."

"Don't like it when it's served back, eh?"

He smiled into his lap. His cupped hands seemed useless and he didn't know what to do with them. Or his words. "You call me when you stop in Atlanta. And when you stop in Charlotte. When you get to D.C."

"I will."

"All three."

"I will!"

"And every day after until I'm satisfied you're not the hostage for some guerilla resistance leader."

She saluted him. "Yes, sir."

"Okay." He said the word for himself. A decisive point, a path to goodbye. *Okay.*

Madeline's arms flew around his neck. Her hot breath burned, but she was real, and she was here, for a few more moments at least.

"I love you, Aggie. Even if you are a big dope."

"Yeah. Yeah, I love you too, Maddy."

"I'll get settled and take the test, I promise."

He nodded but didn't press. She wouldn't take the G.E.D. test. Hard as it was for Augustus to come to acceptance, he accepted it now. The traditional life was not for Madeline Deschanel. The best gift he could give her was the wings to soar.

"Are you sure you don't want me to stay until your friends get here?"

She pulled a candy bar out of her jacket. "Go. Before you change your mind and suck me back into the seventh circle of hell."

Augustus waved at Evangeline. She waved back, blew a kiss to Madeline, then barreled for the door.

He flashed a smile at Maddy. She returned it.

"Merry Christmas!" he called out. She mouthed the words back and waved.

That was the last time he saw her.

CHAPTER 20
The Letter

Charles sat at the old master's chair in the parlor. The grandfather clock in the corner said three, but the thing hadn't run right for years, and he guessed it was closer to four.

He wished he was at Ophélie then. There were two formal offices in the family plantation, one on the ground floor, where most business, public business, was performed. But the third floor was the heir's office. It sat just below the belvedere and overlooked the entire property. From the third floor, you could still see the Mississippi, and to the back, miles and miles of cane fields stretching into the swamp. The office was long enough to have views of both.

As a child, Charles would sit at his father's feet and play with his toys while August sorted through leather books filled with stuff Charles didn't understand. He didn't want to. When he was heir, he would have other people to do the things his mind couldn't comprehend. But those were the whims of a little boy, and he was a man now.

This summer, when he turned twenty-one, he'd make the office his. Maybe take down that old bird painting, the Audubon. Original or not, it was dry and boring, and Charles wanted to transform the office of the heir and bring it into the future. A Black Sabbath poster with a nice gilded frame might do the trick.

But Charles wasn't thinking about Ophélie, or the heir's office. He wasn't thinking about summer. He wasn't even thinking about Madeline, who'd left the house minutes before, maybe for good.

He clutched the letter in his hand. The contents were the real deal. Colin had promised. He'd come through in the end, despite his very strong reservations. He might have even put his future law career at risk to do it, and Charles wouldn't forget that.

He just wasn't sure he could open it.

The door clicked. Colleen slipped in and pressed herself against the wall. "Sorry, I didn't know you were in here."

"It's fine." He rubbed his hands across the stubble dotting his face. "Sit. Whatever."

"I feel terrible. I can't sleep."

"You came to the right party then. Did you remember the beer?"

"I shouldn't..." Colleen perched at the end of the floral print couch. Her neat hair hung half out of whatever she'd had it styled into earlier that evening. The lamp light revealed a drawn, haggard look. It unsettled him, like a piece of furniture out of place. "I shouldn't have said those things. I was mad, but not at her."

"What you said was pretty shitty," he agreed.

She sighed. "Thanks."

"But I said shitty things, and Mama said shitty things. Can we just agree we've all been shitty?" His tired mind wondered if Colleen would play a drinking game with him. *Take a shot every time Charles says shitty.*

Colleen nodded. She smoothed out her wrinkled skirt, but she was a head-to-toe mess and the gesture only accented that. "You're right. When she comes in later, I'll apologize. I'll make it right."

"Oh, she's not coming back."

"She's what?"

"She's not coming back."

"What are you talking about?"

"Augustus drove her to the train station, about..." Charles checked the broken clock. Shrugged. "Evangeline just left, too. Jumped in a taxi."

Colleen's face was wild with incredulity. "What the hell, Charles? Are you serious?" She looked around. "What the hell was Augustus thinking? Are you sure?"

"That's not the kind of thing I'd bother lying about."

She jumped up. "So, why are you still sitting here? We have to go get them!"

"Take a chill pill, Pocahontas. We're not going anywhere."

"What? Why not?"

"Because Augustus did for her what no one else would."

"No one else did it because it's wrong!"

"For you," Charles said. "It's right for her."

"You're not serious."

"Not usually, no," he said. "Tonight, I just happen to be."

"Mama is going to flip her wig when she figures this out!"

"When she wakes up, she won't be happy."

"When she wakes up?"

"Yes, hours from now, Colleen, because we're not gonna wake her to tell her this. If you want to be sorry to Madeline, be sorry. Don't pull a Colleen and ruin this, too."

Her head shook, pulling her messy hair further into chaos. "You're not yourself."

Charles laughed. "Since when has being myself ever been a good thing with you?"

"You really mean to just let her run off? Not finish school?"

Charles swiveled his chair to face her directly. "You say that word, school, like there's nothing more important in the world. I have news for you, Emily Post. Not everyone is you. Not everyone wants your life."

"She won't *have* a life without at least a high school diploma."

"No, Colleen," Charles said quietly. "She won't have your life."

She threw herself back against the couch, apparently defeated. "Now what?"

"Now the world goes on. The sun keeps spinning around the earth—"

"Charles, the sun doesn't... never mind. Hey, what's that in your hand?"

He looked down at the crumpled envelope. "This... it's, uh." He swallowed. Why not? "I got a girl pregnant. Mom paid her off to get rid of it, but she didn't, and I asked Colin to help me track down my daughter."

Colleen whistled her breath out. "I knew about this, Charles. Mama didn't tell me, but Rory did. A daughter. Wow."

"Right. Rory. That prick."

Colleen laughed. "He thought it would win me back. To help me carry the burden, I suppose. Just goes to show he didn't know why I ended it to begin with."

"Why did you?"

"Things here were too complicated. Him telling me my brother got a girl pregnant didn't exactly simplify things."

"You never said anything."

Colleen shrugged. "I don't know, Huck. You've never listened to me, anyway, so what was I going to say? Sometimes the best thing to say is nothing."

Charles clapped his hands together slowly. "Wow, it only took you eighteen years."

She nodded at the letter. "Are you gonna open it?"

"I haven't decided."

"Do you know what's inside?"

Charles turned the manila envelope over in his hands. "An address. I think he got me an address."

"An address to find your daughter."

"Yeah." He set it on the desk. "And then what? If I do, then what?"

"You wanted to know for a reason," Colleen replied. "Do you know what that reason is?"

He threw his hands up. "Yes... no. Hell, I don't know! I don't know, but if I have a kid out there... a little girl... is it right to just fucking ignore it?"

"You really want to know what I think?"

"Yes! For once, I actually give a fuck what you think, Colleen. You're... smarter than me. About shit like this. So?"

Colleen stood up. She twisted her arms in a stretch and stifled a yawn. The night had taken so much out of them all, but no more than her. "I think you need to know exactly what you want before you open that envelope. If you want to be a dad, open it. If you don't, burn it and walk away from this. Choose a path. You can't sit at the trailhead forever. It will eat at you until you can't think clearly anymore."

She paused at the door, and this time, she did yawn. "You know, the fact you're actually conflicted over this says a lot. Maybe you're growing up."

"Fuck's chance of that," he muttered and waved her away.

"Merry Christmas, Huck," she added before the door clicked closed.

Charles traced his finger over the metal fastener on the envelope. Lifted one edge.

If you want to be a dad, open it.

Lifted the other edge. The flap loosened.

If you don't, burn it and walk away from this.

His hand hovered under the flap. He could just slip his hand in, pull out the paper inside. So easy.

But you're a killer. You've taken a life. How can a man who has taken a life be responsible for another?

Charles bent the metal fasteners back into place.

He pressed the envelope to his chest.

It was Christmas.

He'd revisit this tomorrow.

Epilogue: Irish Colleen and the Seven

Colleen Deschanel, known as Irish Colleen to her family and friends, peeked her head into the bedrooms of her seven children on Christmas morning, one by one, as she did every morning of her life.

When she swung the door open into the room of her oldest, Charles, for once he was in it. He squinted a smile up at her. She smiled back and closed the door.

Next, she checked on Augustus, who was awake and at his desk. He didn't turn at the sound of her intrusion, but he wasn't studying. Her son was bent over, hands wound in his short hair. She started to ask the question, but he wouldn't want her to. She moved on, but then something caught her eye.

His bed wasn't empty. Evangeline slept curled in the fetal position in her brother's usual spot. Curious, to see much interaction from these two at all.

Maybe they would tell her about it later.

Colleen slept soundly under a pile of blankets, dead to the world. Irish Colleen hoped her words had been healing rather than hurtful. She only wanted Colleen to be happy. For all her babies to be happy.

She skipped Madeline's room. She wasn't sure why, but she felt a pull to go there last. She needed more time with her middle daughter. There were so many words unsaid, and for so long she'd avoided them, but this was the morning. Today. *No time like the present,* as her mother liked to say.

Maureen was asleep, but she held her hand out at her side, and curled in, the way one might if extending it to another. She blew her an air kiss and moved on.

Elizabeth hadn't been in the hall when Irish Colleen began her pilgrimage, but she was there now. The morning light streamed through the hall window and illuminated her youngest. No sweat or shaking this morning, but the pallor in her skin stopped Irish Colleen in her steps. Her lips, fighting for words, chilled her right to the bone.

And then she remembered.

One of us, one of the seven is going to die at the end of the year and I don't think we can stop it, Mama.

It was December 25. The year was almost at an end.

"Lizzy... Lizzy... don't say it. Don't tell me."

Elizabeth sucked in a jagged breath. "There's someone at the door for you, Mama."

Moments later, a knock sounded.

IRISH COLLEEN WISHED WITH EVERY LAST PIECE OF HER faith that she'd been home alone when the officers came by. By the time she'd let them in, the six of her children that were home—she couldn't bring herself to use the other word—huddled in a mass behind her.

Did they know? Was that part of their witchery, that they knew when one of their own was in danger?

"Mama, no!" Maureen screamed.

Charles tugged her back.

"Mrs. Deschanel?"

"No. I mean, yes, I'm Mrs. Deschanel, but you can't come in.

Whatever you have to tell me, you'll tell me from there, and then you'll leave us!"

The faces of both officers fell, melting into the role this aspect of their job never trained them for. "We received a report of an accident an hour ago, off I-59, near Slidell. A van carrying six people crashed head-on into a city bus."

"The van was carrying a woman we believe is your daughter. Madeline Deschanel," the other officer said, sharing the weight of this load.

"So you talked to her? She's alive?" Evangeline cried from behind.

Maureen howled in agony.

The second officer bowed his head. "Those in the city bus were fine. Minor injuries."

"I don't give a fuck about the city bus!" Charles shouted. "Tell us about Maddy!"

"All but one of the inhabitants of the van were pronounced dead at the scene," he replied, shuffling in place. He held his uniform hat before him like he was already at a funeral. "Madeline was among those who didn't make it. She was gone before we arrived on scene."

Irish Colleen tuned out the screaming behind her. The tears, the shrieks, the desperate clawing between siblings as they struggled to come to terms with this terrible truth.

"What else can you tell me before I close the door?"

"The young woman who survived the wreck, Julie, told us they weren't supposed to be in the van," the first officer said. "They had train tickets, which we found among the wreckage. Headed for D.C., but the train was delayed and she said"—he checked his notes—"Madeline convinced them to talk their friend into driving instead. Julie said Madeline told her she was afraid to go, and if they waited any longer, she might lose her nerve." He reached inside one of his many pockets. "Her bag is at the station in evidence. Just until we can determine if there was a crime involved in the accident. It's standard protocol, nothing to be concerned about. We'll release it to you soon. But I did recover this, and I thought you might want it."

Colleen accepted the piece of paper. There wasn't much to assess. Just two words:

Dear Aggie,

"Julie told the responding officer that Madeline promised to write her brother every day. She took that very seriously, Julie said. He might want… to know, I suppose. I think I would."

The sound that emerged from Augustus was not human. It was not her son. It was…

"Thank you," Irish Colleen managed. Breathing at this moment was no more than an automatic response. If her body was relying on her, she'd be passed out on the floor.

"Here's my card," he said. She took it without being conscious of the action. "I'll personally deliver your daughter's bag with all her belongings as soon as I can, Mrs. Deschanel. You have my word."

"Your word." She set the card on the table beside her. "I have your word, but the Lord has my daughter. Is that about the whole of it?"

"I am so sorry for your loss." He looked past her with heavy, glistening eyes. "For all of your losses. I'm so sorry to be delivering this news to you on Christmas, of all days. God be with you all."

The door closed, and the officers disappeared with their news.

Irish Colleen should turn around. She should face her children. And though their presence in the past moments meant she no longer had to bear the burden of repeating the news, it was her role to comfort them. But if she turned around now, it would be a hollow comfort, for who would comfort her?

How could she ever survive this?

Her Madeline. Maddy. Her troubled child who she'd tried a little less harder than she should have to understand, but ultimately, always, prioritized keeping safe over the less tangible things.

How was she to know the truth in keeping her safe lay in those less tangible things?

Irish Colleen turned around, because she must. Because, in

failing Madeline—who she'd been ready to listen to, later that morning, a Christmas gift of sorts, and now…—she had failed them all. Failed herself. And she must face this.

The haunted, tear-stained faces of all her children filled her heart with darkness, one by one. Colleen and Charles wrapped in one another's arms. Elizabeth pressed into Maureen, who was held up only by the steady arm of her eldest brother. Evangeline clutched Augustus' leg, tearing at it with her hands, sobbing.

But it was in the eyes of Augustus that Irish Colleen saw reflected her true penance.

She'd lost two children that Christmas.

Two years have passed, and the remaining siblings are all dealing with their loss in unhealthy ways. But one of them will pay the ultimate cost.

Don't miss a minute. Download 1972 today.

The Family

Deschanel Family (Line of August)

The Deschanel (*pronounced Day-shah-nell*) family are the line of heirs of the great Charles Deschanel of France, who settled the Deschanel dynasty in Louisiana in 1844. All current day descendants of this original Charles are either of the line of August or Blanche. Deschanels are of the line of August, and all others (Fontenots, Broussards, Guidrys, etc.) come from Blanche. August, with his wife "Irish" Colleen Brady, had seven children: Charles, Augustus, Colleen, Madeline, Evangeline, Maureen, and Elizabeth.

Irish Colleen was August's second wife. His first, Eliza, he married for love, but she was unable to bear children and eventually passed away from cancer.

The rights of inheritance of the Deschanels follow the tradition of the eldest son, so Charles, son of August, is the current heir.

August (1905-1961) & "Irish" Colleen Brady (1932-)

Charles b. 1950

Augustus b. 1951
Colleen b. 1952
Madeline b. 1953
Evangeline b. 1954
Maureen b. 1956
Elizabeth b. 1959

Deschanel-Broussard Family (Line of Blanche)

The Deschanel-Broussard family (*pronounced Brew-sard*), are cousins of the Deschanel family, equal in wealth and prestige. Where the Deschanels are descendants of the line of August, the Broussards are descendants of the line of Blanche. Claudius Broussard is Blanche's third husband, and the children from this union are considered her most favored. She also has a son by her second husband, Johnson Guidry, but her relationship with Pierce is fractured.

Blanche did not have children by her first husband, Ellis Kenner. Both Ellis Kenner and Johnson Guidry died of "mysterious circumstances."

Blanche Deschanel (b. 1906) & Johnson Guidry (1890-1930)
Pierce b. 1926

& Claudius Broussard (b. 1900)
Eugenia b. 1940
Pierce b. 1926
Cassius b. 1942
Wyatt (1943-1955)
Noble (1944-1955)

Guidry Family (Line of Blanche)

The Guidry family are those descended from Pierce Guidry, first son of Blanche Deschanel-Broussard. Although the first son is the heir on the Deschanel side, Blanche does not recognize Pierce as her heir. Instead, she's chosen her second child and eldest daughter, Eugenia Fontenot. Pierce represents his line of the family as one of the seven Deschanel Magi Collective Council. His two daughters, Pansy and Kitty, are also on the Council.

Of Pierce's children, only Pansy, so far, is married.

The Guidrys, mainly due to Blanche's disdain for her second husband, Johnson, are considered the black sheep of the clan. Pierce's choice in a wife, Winnifred Babin, has further emphasized this message, due to her background as a trapper's daughter and connection to voodoo.

Pierce Guidry (b. 1926) & Winnifred Babin (b. 1926)

Pansy b. 1949 (m. Placide Lafont b. 1945)
Alton b. 1950
Kitty b. 1954

Fontenot Family (Line of Blanche)

The Fontenot family are those descended from Eugenia Broussard-Fontenot, second daughter of Blanche Deschanel-Broussard. Although Eugenia is a second child, and a daughter to boot, Blanche recognizes Eugenia as her heir. Eugenia is married to Wallace Fontenot, and they have three sons. Eugenia represents her line of the family as one of the seven Deschanel Magi Collective Council.

The Fontenots are well-respected in the community, with a similar prestige as their Deschanel cousins.

Eugenia Broussard (b. 1940) & Wallace Fontenot (b. 1939)
Luther b. 1962
Llewellyn b. 1963
Lowell b. 1964

Broussard Family (Line of Blanche)

The Broussard family are those descended from Cassius, third child and second son of Blanche Deschanel-Broussard. Cassius is married to Helene Barrow, and they have two children, a son and a daughter. Cassius represents his line of the family as one of the seven Deschanel Magi Collective Council.

The Broussards, like the Fontenots, are well-respected in the community, with a similar prestige as their Deschanel cousins.

Cassius Broussard (b. 1942) & Helene Barrow (b. 1944)
Jasper b. 1963
Imogen b. 1965

Sullivan Family

The Sullivans are one of the oldest and most trusted families in New Orleans. A family of attorneys, a majority of Sullivans, most notably males until recently, join the family law firm, Sullivan & Associates, which has been a New Orleans staple since 1839. The family came up through the ranks, by their bootstraps, with humble beginnings as Irish immigrant laborers. The Sullivans are both the attorneys and friends of the Deschanel Family. Like the Deschanels, the designation of heir follows the eldest son, and so Colin Sullivan Sr. is considered the head of the family. His father, Patrick, still lives, but in quiet retirement.

Colin Sullivan Sr. (b. 1932) & Josephine Bartleby (b. 1931)

Colin Sullivan Jr. b. 1950
Rory Sullivan b. 1952
Patrick Sullivan b. 1953
Chelsea Sullivan b. 1956

Sullivan & Associates

Sullivan & Associates is a family-owned law firm, and one of the oldest and most trusted in New Orleans, founded in 1839 by Aidan Sullivan. Comprised mostly of Sullivans, the firm is considered something of a birthright for any Sullivans looking to go into law. They have represented the Deschanel interests for over a century. Charles Deschanel's best friend, Colin Sullivan Jr., as well as Colin's two brothers, Rory and Patrick, all plan to join the family firm one day. Colin Sullivan Sr. is the current Senior Partner, following the retirement of his father, Patrick. Colin Sr. and his brothers, Jerome and Jamie, are the figureheads of the firm.

Homes & Properties

Oak Haven

The old Victorian mansion Irish Colleen and her seven children reside in, on Chestnut and Sixth in the Garden District, just beyond Lafayette Cemetery No. 1. Although there are larger (Magnolia Grace) and more storied (Ophélie) homes in the family possession, August Deschanel chose this particular property to raise his family in with the thought of giving them a more "normal" upbringing than he had.

The Gardens

The colossal mansion of Ophelia Deschanel at Jackson Ave., taking up an entire square block between Coliseum and Prytania in the Garden District. The Gardens also houses the cavernous chambers where the Deschanel Magi Collective and the Collective Council meet to discuss family business. The architectural style of the estate is Italianate, and the most notable feature is the extensive, exotic garden wrapping around the property, shielding the home from outside view. This house will be inherited by the future Deschanel Magi Collective Magistrate.

Ophélie

A large plantation and surrounding lands purchased by Charles Deschanel I, built in 1844, and currently occupied intermittently by the Deschanel family. Charles will inherit the property as the heir to the estate. Located near Vacherie, an hour west of New Orleans, the Greek Revival ivory mansion on the Mississippi River is secluded from the road by gates and foliage. The estate has forty-five rooms and large ornate gardens, as well as two hundred outbuildings from when the property was a working plantation.

Magnolia Grace

A beautiful, traditional Greek Revival mansion in the Garden District that once belonged to Fitz Deschanel (the second son of Charles I), and has ever since been passed down through the second sons. Augustus Deschanel is set to inherit this property, which is located on Prytania, near Eighth.

Femme Forte

A sprawling Northshore mansion along Lake Pontchartrain, considered the birthright of Blanche and her descendants. The property will be inherited by Eugenia Fontenot, her favorite child.

Weatherly Estate

The vast, columned Uptown home of Daniel Weatherly Sr., gifted for his patronage of Tulane. His son, Dan Jr., is a good friend of Charles Deschanel. The estate is located near the sister universities of Tulane and Loyola, by the Ursuline's Academy.

Also by Sarah M. Cradit

KINGDOM OF THE WHITE SEA

Kingdom of the White Sea Trilogy

The Kingless Crown

The Broken Realm

The Hidden Kingdom

The Book of All Things

Blackwood Cycle

The Raven and the Rush

The Poison and the Paladin

Southerlands Cycle

The Sylvan and the Sand

The Flame and the Forsaken

Guardians Cycle

The Altruist and the Assassin

The Belle and the Blackbird

Darkwood Cycle

The Melody and the Master

The Hand and the Heart

Sceptre Cycle

The Claw and the Crowned

The Duke and the Disciple

THE SAGA OF CRIMSON & CLOVER

The House of Crimson and Clover Series

The Storm and the Darkness

Shattered

The Illusions of Eventide

Bound

Midnight Dynasty

Asunder

Empire of Shadows

Myths of Midwinter

The Hinterland Veil

The Secrets Amongst the Cypress

Within the Garden of Twilight

House of Dusk, House of Dawn

Midnight Dynasty Series

A Tempest of Discovery

A Storm of Revelations

A Torrent of Deceit

The Seven Series

Nineteen Seventy

Nineteen Seventy-Two

Nineteen Seventy-Three

Nineteen Seventy-Four

Nineteen Seventy-Five

Nineteen Seventy-Six

Nineteen Eighty

Vampires of the Merovingi Series

The Island

and more

The Dusk Trilogy

St. Charles at Dusk: The Story of Oz and Adrienne

Flourish: The Story of Anne Fontaine

Banshee: The Story of Giselle Deschanel

Crimson & Clover Stories

Available as a single collection, The Shorts

Surrender: The Story of Oz and Ana

Shame: The Story of Jonathan St. Andrews

Fire & Ice: The Story of Remy & Fleur

Dark Blessing: The Landry Triplets

Pandora's Box: The Story of Jasper & Pandora

The Menagerie: Oriana's Den of Iniquities

A Band of Heather: The Story of Colleen and Noah

The Ephemeral: The Story of Autumn & Gabriel

Bayou's Edge: The Landry Triplets

For more information, and exciting bonus material, visit www.sarahmcradit.com

About the Author

Sarah is the USA Today and International Bestselling Author of over forty contemporary and epic fantasy stories, and the creator of the Kingdom of the White Sea and Saga of Crimson & Clover universes.

Born a geek, Sarah spends her time crafting rich and multilayered worlds, obsessing over history, playing her retribution paladin (and sometimes destruction warlock), and settling provocative Tolkien debates, such as why the Great Eagles are not Gandalf's personal taxi service. Passionate about travel, she's been to over twenty countries collecting sparks of inspiration, and is always planning her next adventure.

Sarah and her husband live in a beautiful corner of SE Pennsylvania with their three tiny benevolent pug dictators.

www.sarahmcradit.com

www.ingramcontent.com/pod-product-compliance
Lightning Source LLC
Chambersburg PA
CBHW020334310726
48979CB00015B/2363/J

* 9 7 8 1 9 5 8 7 4 4 2 4 6 *